THE
CHRONICLES OF
BELTESHAZZAR

ALSO BY DAVID LANTZ

Fiction

The Sword of the Scroll

The Brotherhood of the Scroll

Non-Fiction

The Unraveling of We the People

Think Like Jesus, Lead Like Moses: Leadership Lessons from the Wilderness Crucible

Online Courses — Christian Study/Leadership

Clash of the Superpowers: A Comparative History Curriculum Accompanying The Brotherhood of the Scroll

Think Like Jesus, Lead Like Moses

Pursuing Your Mission from God

Online Courses — Online Teaching

How to Teach with Technology Online

How to Teach Online 24/7/365

For more information about books and courses by David Lantz, visit his website at https://wisejargon.com/leadership/

THE
CHRONICLES OF
BELTESHAZZAR

DAVID LANTZ

The Chronicles of Belteshazzar

ISBN: 978-1-7376114-0-0 (Paperback, Ingram Spark)
ISBN: 978-1-7376114-1-7 (Hardback, Ingram Spark)
ISBN: 978-1-7376114-2-4 (E-book)
ISBN: 978-1-7376114-3-1 (Paperback, Amazon)

Library of Congress Control Number: 2021918529

Cover Design by Shelley Savoy.

Cover photo credit : The cover image is made from images in the public domain taken from Wikimedia Commons, King David by Guercino, Tower by Valkenbroch, Daniel by Giovanni Dall'orto, Lions by Sir Peter Paul Rubens, and Landscape by Thomas Doughty.

Interior design by Booknook.biz

www.wisejargon.com

To order additional copies of this book, contact:

David L. Lantz, dlantz@wisejargon.com or visit www.wisejargon.com/chronicles
Indianapolis, Indiana

*To the Grand Children. Born, yet to be born, and adopted
into the family. Love you, always.*

Table of Contents

Acknowledgements

No one takes on a book project like this without help, and I am no exception. First, I would like to thank friends and family who participated in allowing me to photograph them as various characters in the book. My son Josh Lantz (Babylonian Soldier/Naaman) and his wife Kasha Lantz (Timnah); Ed Miller, Kasha's father (Wiseman / Haman), and her brother Jonathan Miller (Daniel). Additionally, thanks to Ben Bruemmer (Servant) and his wife Mary Bruemmer for opening their home to allow us to take pictures there, and thanks to Michael Deason for posing as Nebuchadnezzar. While their pictures may not appear in the novel itself, I will be incorporating them into social media posts in some fashion.

Several people read earlier drafts of the book and provided their feedback. That includes Mary Bruemmer, who is a fifth-grade teacher, as well as three special young people: Isaiah Lantz, Nadia O'Neil and Hope Van Deman. Their input and perspective were invaluable to me in thinking through the interaction between Grandpa and the children.

Much thanks to Shelley Savoy who did a fantastic job in taking my ideas to produce the cover design and artwork. And, a HUGE thinks to Kimberly Hitchens and her team at BooknookBiz for their excellent work and patience in working with me!

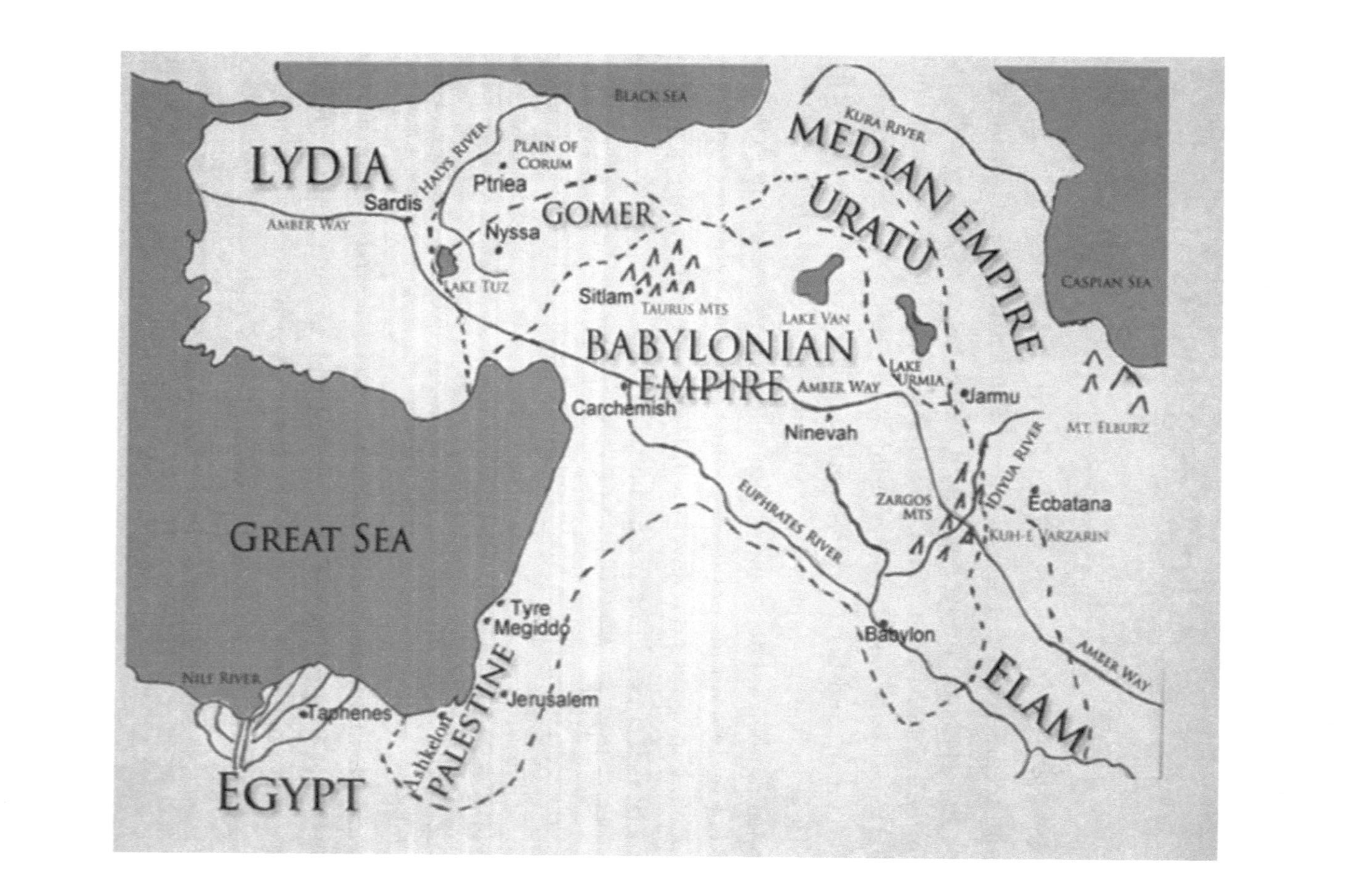

LYDIA
BLACK SEA
KURA RIVER
MEDIAN EMPIRE
PLAIN OF CORUM
Ptriea
Sardis
HALYS RIVER
AMBER WAY
Nyssa
GOMER
URATU
CASPIAN SEA
LAKE TUZ
Sitlam
TAURUS MTS
LAKE VAN
BABYLONIAN
EMPIRE
LAKE URMIA
AMBER WAY
Jarmu
MT. ELBURZ
Carchemish
Ninevah
EUPHRATES RIVER
ZARGOS MTS
IDIYLA RIVER
Ecbatana
KUH-E YARZARIN
GREAT SEA
Tyre
Megiddo
Babylon
AMBER WAY
NILE RIVER
Jerusalem
Taphenes
Ashkelon
PALESTINE
ELAM
EGYPT

Prologue

ISAIAH WALKED THE school hallway, his destination in plain sight. It had been nearly two weeks since the incident. Would she remember?

Good. Her locker was open, the door facing him. He snuck right up so he'd be standing there when she shut it. Isaiah stepped into position, checked his hair. And waited.

The locker door shut.

"Hi, Mary," Isaiah said before she could say something snarky. She looked at him with her big brown eyes, her long brown hair tied in a single braid hanging almost to her waist. He stood a good three inches taller than her – and she seemed frozen looking up at him. Isaiah didn't waste any time, and said, "I figured out some things about what you said the other day."

Mary blinked at him. Twice. "Wha … What are you talking about, Isaiah?" She finally stammered out.

Isaiah grew more confident. This was going better than he had hoped. "Oh, you know. The other day, you grabbed my Gideon's Bible out of my hands, and when I started chasing you, you threw it in some bushes and yelled 'separation between church and state'."

"Oh, that." Mary replied. And then, with more fire in her eyes, she tilted her head, looked up at him and said, "So what does it mean, Mr. Smarty Pants? Did you have to google it?" Mary folded her arms as she held a copy of <u>The Hunger Games </u>she was reading.

Isaiah shook his head. "Nope. Better than that. My grandpa told me about it when he explained the Chronicles of Belteshazzar."

"The Chronicles of who? Belta-Shoe-Carnival?"

"Belteshazzar." Isaiah struggled to not let himself get upset. "That was the Babylonian name of Daniel. You know, the Daniel in the Lions' Den Daniel from the bible." Isaiah was quickly losing his confidence. Maybe Auntie Dr. Sarah had been wrong, after all?

Mary's eyes lit up, and the freckles on her face became swallowed up in the creases of her mischievous smile. "Does your grandpa tell interesting stories?"

Isaiah grinned. "Oh, yah! There's sword fighting, secret coded messages, stories of ancient gods, and even some romance. Not a lot, but some! If you like, I can tell it to you over a coke or something." This was the moment of truth. What would she say?

Mary closed and locked her locker. Turning her head to look at him over her shoulder, she said, "I'll meet you at the soda shop after school and you can buy me a milkshake and tell me all about it. Deal?"

"Deal!" Said Isaiah. Mary waved, turned the other direction, and headed off to class. Isaiah stood there, and wondered to himself – did he have enough money in his wallet for a milkshake?

CHAPTER 1

Auntie Dr. Sarah

DR. SARAH MICHELLE Pierce sat on a park bench as her brother Jason's four children - Isaiah, Nadia, Josiah and Hope played nearby. It was a fall day in mid-September. The leaves were just beginning to turn color. It was a time of year she always enjoyed in her hometown of Indianapolis. As the song went, it was good to be "back home in Indiana."

Sarah returned her eyes to her bible. It was open to Daniel Chapter 6. She began to read verse one:

It pleased Darius to appoint 120 satraps to rule throughout the kingdom, with three administrators over them, one of whom was Daniel.

But just as she began her reading, two hands covered both her eyes.

"Guess who!" Squeaked a high-pitched voice that trailed off with a slight crack at the end of the question. There was no hiding the fact that her twelve-year-old nephew would soon experience a deepening in his voice as he approached his teen age years.

"Well," said Sarah, "it can't be Josiah or Hope because they're not tall enough to reach my eyes!" At five feet nine inches, Auntie Dr. Sarah, as her nieces and nephews called her, even when sitting, was too tall for either of her two younger nephews, seven and five years old respectively, to easily reach.

"And it's not me!" announced a confident ten-year-old Nadia. Of the four children, her dark hair and olive skin color most reminded anyone looking at them of their father, Jason. It was a hair and skin color combination that Auntie Dr. Sarah shared with her younger brother.

"Well," announced Sarah in her most authoritative surgeon's voice, "that can only leave one other person who has his hands over my eyes. It's …. Isaiah!" She announced this conclusion as, with one motion, she put her bible down on the park bench she was sitting on and pulled her oldest nephew around in front of her.

"How did you know I didn't pick Hope up and have her put her hands over your eyes?" said Isaiah.

"Because he's with Josiah over there going up and down the slide, silly," replied Auntie Dr. Sarah as she pointed in Hope's direction.

The second grader looked up when she heard her name, and saw her aunt motioning in her direction. Josiah grabbed Hope, and the two younger children came over to join their older siblings to see what they were talking about. Unlike Nadia, both Josiah's and Hope's hair was sandy brown, like that of their mother's. Josiah's skin was darker than Isaiah's, while Hope's was fair like her oldest brother's.

For his part, twelve-year-old Isaiah towered over his younger siblings at five foot seven inches. Always tall for his age (he was very proud of the fact that he was nearly at the 90th percentile for his age), his other distinguishing characteristic was that he had dark red hair. This was a curious genetic trick that God had played on his own paternal grandmother, who was one hundred percent Chinese.

"Auntie Dr. Sarah," said Isaiah as he decided to sit beside his aunt, "do you know what happened to me at school yesterday?"

"No, because you haven't told me," replied his Aunt. "What happened?"

"Well, you remember how I told you two people came to school last week to hand out Gideon Bibles to whomever wanted one? Well, I was outside during lunch yesterday and I was flipping through my Gideon Bible that I got. It has REALLY small print! I was looking for a story from the Old Testament, but just when I figured out that it was only a New Testament bible, plus proverbs and the psalms, a girl named Mary came along, ripped it out of my hands, and yelled 'Separation of Church and State' while she ran off with my bible."

"What did you do, Isaiah?" asked Nadia. "Did you chase after her?"

"Yes, I did. When I started to catch up with her, she threw my bible in some bushes. I stopped to get it, and she ran off to a group of her friends."

"Did you tell the teacher? I would have told the teacher!" stated an emphatic Josiah.

"No," answered Isaiah. "I wasn't sure if I was doing something that was wrong." Isaiah looked down at his feet, and then back up at his aunt. "Auntie Dr. Sarah, do you think I was doing something that was wrong, reading my bible at school?"

Absolutely NOT," she replied. "You know, when your dad and I were very small, Grandpa used to have us act out bible stories. One of those stories was Daniel in the Lions' Den."

Nadia perked right up at the mention of the story. "I know about that story! Didn't he get thrown in jail because he prayed to God?"

"Yes, that's right – only the jail was the den where the lions lived," replied Aunt Sarah. "Say, aren't you kids going to spend next weekend with Grandpa and Nai Nai?"

"Yes, we are!" said Josiah excitedly. "We're going to camp out in the Sunroom. Grandpa always sleeps with us!"

Sarah extended her long arms and pulled the four close to her. In a hushed but excited voice, she smiled and said: "Well, you should ask Grandpa to tell you the story of all the adventures Daniel had. The Prophet Daniel lived in a time when very few people believed the Word of God. Grandpa loves to talk about that kind of thing. Would you like him to tell you stories about how Daniel had to deal with people who didn't believe in God?"

"Can we eat popcorn and stay up real late?" Josiah bounced up and down as he waited for Auntie Dr. Sarah to answer.

"You know, I am pretty sure that if Nai Nai says yes, then Grandpa will say yes too! Tell you what, I'll talk to Grandpa so that he can get everything ready. Ok?"

"Will you be there too?" asked Nadia.

Aunt Sarah gave the top of Nadia's head a quick brushing and answered, "No, I have to work at the hospital this weekend. It's my turn to be in surgery rotation to fix people up when they get hurt. But I'll expect you all to tell me all about it when I see you next time!"

Aunt Sarah looked at her watch. "Well, guys, it's time to go home. I promised your mom and dad I'd have you back in time to wash up for supper. Come on, my car is parked over there."

As the children followed their aunt to her car, Isaiah realized he'd forgotten to ask what the phrase "separation of church and state" meant. He hoped he would remember to ask Grandpa when they saw him next.

CHAPTER 2

When Praying was against the Law!

Isaiah, Nadia, Josiah, and Hope's parents drove away. Their Grandmother Pierce stood behind them as they waved goodbye. However, they didn't call her Grandmother Pierce. Or Grandma. No, she had a special name.

Nai Nai.

Nai Nai is the Chinese name for the grandmother who is the father's mother. Nai Nai was their daddy's mom, and she was Chinese. She was very smart, very funny, very organized and always had something fun planned for her grandchildren.

"Your Grandpa and I have really been looking forward to having you spend the weekend with us," said Nai Nai as the car drove out of sight.

The children looked at her. Isaiah scratched his head, and, looking at Nai Nai with a frown on his face, said: "Auntie Dr. Sarah said I should ask Grandpa about how, when the prophet Daniel was alive, they passed a law that said he shouldn't pray to God."

"Yes, Aunt Sarah told me about that. We've made some special plans for Grandpa to tell you a story tonight to explain that. But first, I have a question."

What, Nai Nai?" asked Nadia.

"Does anyone want pizza for dinner?"

Isaiah, Nadia and Josiah screamed "Yes! Yes!" While his older siblings were screaming for pizza, Hope raised her hand.

"Quiet, kids, Hope has a question." After the other children quieted down, Nai Nai asked, "Now, what's your question, Hope?"

"Nai Nai, may we please have ice cream for dessert?"

Nai Nai beamed a smile. "Why yes, Hope, you may!" Right after she said that, Nai Nai looked up and pointed at a car driving up to the house. "Look, kids. There's Grandpa. He's got the pizza. Let's go inside, wash our hands, and get ready to eat!"

Dinner was spent with the children telling their grandparents about everything they'd done since last they'd gotten together. As Nai Nai served everyone ice cream, Isaiah told his grandparents about how the girl at school had taken his Gideon bible and yelled that reading it at school was against "separation of church and state." After telling Grandpa about what had happened, he asked his question: "What does that mean – 'Separation of church and state'?"

"That's a great question, Isaiah," replied Grandpa. "Now, you know that I'm a college professor – that's what I do for a living, right?"

"Yes, Grandpa. That's why I figured you'd be able to tell me what it means."

"Good. Now, what you should know is that I have two ways of explaining things. One way is asking questions. The other is telling stories. Right now, I want to answer your question by asking you some questions. Then, later this evening, I want to tell you and your brothers a story." Grandpa looked into his oldest grandson's wide open eyes, spooned his last bite of ice cream into his mouth and added, "Deal, Isaiah?"

"Deal, Grandpa!"

"Ok, Isaiah. Here's the first question: Do you remember the story of Daniel in the Lion's Den?"

"Yes! We were just talking about that with Auntie Dr. Sarah a few days ago."

"Well, isn't that something," said Grandpa. "So you know that there were people in Babylon who hated the prophet Daniel so much they decided to trap him because of his religion."

"Yes – they knew he prayed regularly to God, so they passed a law that made it a crime to pray to anyone but King Nebuchadnezzar for a whole month. But Daniel went ahead and prayed to God anyway, so they arrested him and had him thrown into the lions' den."

Grandpa smiled at his eldest grandson. "Very good! Now, when the United States became a country, there was a lot of discussion about what laws the government could and could not make. An important topic had to do with religion. And so, there were a set of ten changes made to the Constitution that we call the Bill of Rights. The first of those ten changes – we call them the Ten Amendments – said that Congress may not pass any laws that restrict our freedom of religion. And that brings me to where I want to answer your question about 'separation of church and state.' Now, do you know who Thomas Jefferson was?"

"He wrote the Declaration of Independence, and he was the third President of the United States!"

"Very good, Isaiah! Now, here's where things get sort of complicated. There was a group of Christians in the State of Connecticut – the Danbury Baptist Association – who wrote a letter to President Jefferson. They reminded him that in the Declaration of Independence that he wrote back at the start of the

> It was not until **Everson v. Board of Education** (1947) that Jefferson's words "separation between church and state" found their way into a Supreme Court ruling. In the case, Justice Hugo Black wrote: "In the words of Jefferson, the clause against establishment of religion by law was intended to erect "a wall of separation between Church and State."
>
> Over time, many people have come to believe the concept of "separation between church and state" is part of the First Amendment. In fact, It was first mentioned in a letter from President Thomas Jefferson in his 1802 reply to a question from the Danbury Baptist association of Connecticut.

Revolutionary War, it says that God, not man, gives all people their rights. Among those rights is the right to worship God and practice our religion as God leads us to do."

"The Baptists in Danbury Connecticut believed that since God gave them the right to worship Him, they wanted to know how the government could give them the same right again? And if the government believed it could grant the freedom of religion to Americans, couldn't politicians in the future change the Constitution to say that freedom of religion was no longer allowed?"

It took a moment for Isaiah to digest what Grandpa had just said. But then, his eyes grew wide, and he said "Wow, Grandpa. You mean the people could someday come along and say that praying to God was against the law?"

"Exactly, Isaiah," said Grandpa as he sat down beside his grandson. It was just the two of them now, as Nai Nai had taken the other kids to another part of the house. "And so, President Jefferson wrote the Danbury Baptists a reply letter and said that the First Amendment was intended to act as a 'wall of separation between church and state.' He meant it as a one-way wall that would keep government from ever taking away peoples' right to worship God as they wished."

"But I don't think that's what Mary meant when she grabbed the bible out of my hands, Grandpa."

Yes, you're right, Isaiah," replied Grandpa. "You see, there came a time when some people wanted to get God out of the schools. They wanted to get people to stop believing in God. Believing in Jesus. And so, they did exactly what the Danbury Baptists had been afraid of. Starting in the 1940s, the Supreme Court started to use Jefferson's comment about a "wall of separation between church and state" to rule that the government needed to be protected from the churches.

"And so what does that mean about people like Mary doing what she did?"

"You know, Isaiah, adults can sometimes act strangely. About one hundred years ago, some very influential people started to change the way school children were taught about all of this. And so, today, many people think that you can't have a bible in places like a school, or even say a prayer. Mary didn't know any better. She'd just been taught something that wasn't right, and she believes it."

"Auntie Dr. Sarah said that's sort of what happened to the Prophet Daniel," said Isaiah. "Is that right?"

"Yes, it is. And that leads me to my other favorite way of teaching – telling stories!" answered Grandpa.

Just then, Nai Nai walked into the kitchen. "Isaiah, your brothers have finished with their baths. Why don't you go take yours now? Then, Grandpa will tell all of you the story of the prophet Daniel. Ok?"

"Can we eat popcorn while he tells us the story?"

"Of course! I'll make some popcorn when you finish your bath," replied Nai Nai. "Now, off you go!"

Isaiah got up to go take his bath while Grandpa cleaned off the dishes and put them in the dishwasher.

CHAPTER 3

The Story Begins

NADIA AND JOSIAH were already in the Sunroom when Isaiah walked in fresh and clean from his bath. Nai Nai had taken Hope down the hall to build a castle with some Legos, as she and Grandpa both knew that she wouldn't last for story time. As the three children settled in, Grandpa faced them, his back to the sunroom windows that let in lots of sunlight during the day. The children could see the sun setting through the large windows.

Josiah and Nadia sat on a small couch against the wall, with two armchairs on either side of the couch. Isaiah scrambled into the chair furthest from the door to the room. Nai Nai came in right behind him with popcorn and sodas for everyone.

Grandpa had a flannel board on which were several characteristics. On one wall was a map of the ancient middle east. On another wall were pictures of mountains and an ancient city with funny looking pyramids called Ziggurats. On a podium in front of Grandpa was an ancient looking book. As he turned to face his grandchildren, Grandpa held the book up to show it to the kids.

"All right," said Grandpa. "I know you've all read the story of the Prophet Daniel in the lions' den in the bible. What I want to do tonight is present you with a sort of play. We'll use characters on the flannel board. We'll use bible verses. But we'll also use our imaginations to think about what life was like in those days. This special book that I have in front of me will help to transport us back to the time of the Prophet Daniel. It is a special book, and this is the only copy in the world. Do you know what the book is called?"

All three shook their heads no, eyes fixed on their grandfather. Josiah was the only one who spoke up. "What's the book called, Grandpa?"

"It's called The Chronicles of Belteshazzar!" intoned Grandpa as he raised his arms and looked up to the ceiling. "And through the magic in this book, we will be transported to the time of the Prophet Daniel to see, hear and smell all that happened to him!"

"I hope Daniel didn't fart like you fart, Grandpa!" Josiah blurted out. Nadia glared at her younger brother, as she didn't feel such language was appropriate.

"I think I'm going to go check on Hope now and leave the four of you to the story," said Nai Nai as she left the room while trying to stifle a laugh.

Acting as though he'd not heard Josiah's comment, Grandpa walked over to the map of the ancient middle east on the sunroom wall. "Three thousand, six hundred and five years ago, a really important battle was fought at a place called Carchemish. It was on the Euphrates River north of the nation of Israel. It was on an ancient trade route that the Italian explorer Marco Polo traveled when he journeyed to China in the 1270s A.D. A.D. stands for 'Anno Domine,' which is a Latin phrase that means 'In the Year of Our Lord'."

Grandpa walked back to the flannel board and pulled out several figures to put on the board. "Now, there were two nations that were involved in the battle at Carchemish in the year 605 B.C. B.C stands for 'Before Christ.' The Assyrians had controlled this part of the world for nearly one hundred years, but they had been conquered by Egypt. Pharaoh Necho, the King of Egypt, had come to fight off the invading Babylonian Army that was commanded by Nebuchadnezzar. There was a terrible battle that was fought there. The Babylonians defeated the Egyptians and their Assyrian allies. Pharaoh Necho and what was left of his army fled south back to Egypt. With the Egyptian army defeated, no one was able to stand against the invading Babylonians."

Grandpa took down the commanders of the Assyrians, Egyptians and Babylonians, and put up a picture of Jerusalem and her king, Jehoiakim. And then, he moved a picture of an army up beside the walls of Jerusalem. "News of the Babylonians spread throughout Palestine. Now Jehoiakim was the King of Judah, and he lived in Jerusalem. One day, the Babylonian army showed up outside the walls of Jerusalem. And guess what happened?"

All the children were chewing on their popcorn. Isaiah looked at the picture of Jerusalem, the Babylonian army and King Jehoiakim standing at the wall. He loved hearing about battles and wars. "What, Grandpa?"

With a smile on his face, Grandpa raised his finger to signal that they must wait a moment, and then left the room.

CHAPTER 4

King Jehoiakim Surrenders

LESS THAN A minute after Grandpa had left the room, he came back in dressed as an ancient Wiseman. Grandpa had put on a beard, a head scarf and royal robe like the kids had seen people use to dress up as one of the Three Wise Men for Christmas plays. Standing before them, Grandpa opened The Chronicles of Belteshazzar and began to read:

In the third year of Jehoiakim, King of Judah, the Lord God raised up a Lion from the east, one Nebuchadnezzar. In that same year, King Nebuchadnezzar led Babylon at a place called Carchemish, and there defeated the Egyptians. Though he did so in the name of his god, Marduk, the king of the Babylonian gods, the God of the Hebrews had in fact ordained his steps. Nebuchadnezzar's comings and goings were prophesied by the Voice of the Lord, Jeremiah of Anathoth. Here begins the account of how the God of the Universe caused the Children of Israel to go in exile to the land of the Chaldeans. My name is Belteshazzar, and this is my story.

The Chronicles of Belteshazzar

"Sire, your presence is required at the Gate of Benjamin!" exclaimed a guard as he burst in on King Jehoiakim and those meeting with him. They looked at him, not in surprise, but in resignation to the event unfolding outside the city walls.

"I am coming," replied Jehoiakim in an irritated, whining voice. Curse Jeremiah! If not for him and his incessant prophecies about the destruction of Jerusalem, he would be sure of his course. But now, instead of showing his people that he, the King, was in command of the situation, he was being made to look a groveling fool. He glanced nervously at his generals and temple priests. Was that a look of sadistic pleasure he saw in their eyes at the thought that he must face the Babylonians? He looked at the guard as he rose from his chair.

"I said I am coming!" Jehoiakim snapped. "Tell me, is Nebuchadnezzar at their head? How many soldiers? What are their demands?"

The guard had turned and was leading Jehoiakim and his entourage out of the palace toward the Gate of Benjamin. As they strode toward their destination, the guard turned his head to speak back over his shoulder. "It doesn't appear that Nebuchadnezzar is with them. They appear to have a force of 15,000 soldiers and await your arrival to deliver their surrender terms to us."

Jehoiakim walked in silence with the guard and his advisors the rest of the way to the city gates. He had received reports that Nebuchadnezzar's main army was still several day's march from Jerusalem. Clearly, he was coming, and those outside the city were but the vanguard of the larger invading force. He thought about their defenses. The walls of the city were six feet thick and twenty-five feet high. Since the time of King David, Jerusalem had withstood

> **The Kings – Who Are They**
>
> **Jehoiakim** was king of Judah from 609 to 598 BC. He was the son of King Josiah.
>
> **Necho II** of Egypt was Pharaoh from 610–595 BC. Necho oversaw many construction projects.
>
> **Nebuchadnezzar II** was king of Babylon 605–562 BC. His father, Nabopolassar, ruled Babylon from 626–605 BC.
>
> **Zedekiah** was king of Judah from 597 to 586 B.C. He was the second son of King Josiah, and the half-brother of King Jehoiakim.

the tests of time and many adversaries. Though not impregnable, it presented no easy prey to any army wishing to sack her. But the Babylonians were different. Master builders themselves, they were well known for their ability to efficiently lay siege to a city and penetrate its defenses.

Jehoiakim mounted the steps leading to the guard house on the western side of the gate. When he looked out at the invading army, his eyes became fixed on the spectacle before him, causing him to turn white with fear. There, in a line just out of bow shot, twelve of his soldiers hung from stakes planted in the ground, killed by the Babylonians. Regaining his composure, he looked out at the Babylonian representatives standing under a flag of truce.

He steeled himself for the confrontation. "I am Jehoiakim, Son of Josiah, King of Judah. What is it you seek?"

"Babylon has defeated Egypt at Carchemish," began the messenger. "As you have paid tribute to Egypt, so now you will pay tribute to Babylon. This is not all. You will send out 1,500 of your ruling class - teachers, architects, and artisans. These shall be taken to Babylon and trained in our ways. If you fail to comply with our demands, we shall burn this city to the ground. You have three days to comply with these demands, issued by Naaman, Captain of the Imperial guard. Resistance is futile."

Jehoiakim watched as the messenger turned and led his men back into the fold of the main army. That was it. No discussion. No negotiation – surrender, or die.

"You can not give in to them, King Jehoiakim," Shemaiah, one of his court prophets, said. Other heads nodded.

"The Lord will not allow His temple to be destroyed - so it is written in the Torah," Pashur added. "All that is needed is for you to be strong and courageous. God will overcome our enemies."

Jehoiakim glared at the "holy man." It wasn't their necks that were on the line. "How can God protect us? Did he protect Josiah my father from the Egyptians? No! They killed him, and we were forced to pay tribute to them. Now an army greater than Egypt's is here. And you tell me to be strong and courageous? You are a fool!"

"My king, we have three days," replied Hananiah. A rival of Jeremiah, Hananiah was one of the few prophets that Jehoiakim trusted. "God may yet provide. If he does not rescue us, you can do as you see best at that time."

Jehoiakim saw a way to save face, and took it. "Yes, yes, that is what we shall do! Let us return to our chambers and pray." Long ago, Jehoiakim had learned when it was convenient to sound pious. Now was one of those times. As they walked back to the royal chambers, Jehoiakim made plans to have a list of Hebrews drawn up to hand over to the Babylonians. He smiled to himself as he thought further, and realized this was truly a blessing in disguise. With one deft move, Jehoiakim would exile most, if not all, of his potential enemies and their supporters to Babylon! He had paid tribute to Egypt, so now he would pay Babylon - in essence, no difference from an economic point of view. And, thanks to the prattling of Jeremiah, he could convince the people that he was in fact doing God's will!

Jehoiakim couldn't wait to draw up the list of Hebrews to be exiled.

CHAPTER 5

Exile to Babylon

NAAMAN'S COMMAND FORMED lines five rows deep. Between the two lines, palm branches had been laid. King Nebuchadnezzar and his escort rounded a bend in the road and emerged from the shadow of a hill obstructing any view of the main army from the waiting corps. On cue, trumpets blew and the men cheered the arrival of their king.

Nebuchadnezzar and Naaman were accompanied by Shamgar, general of the Eastern army. The three men went into Naaman's tent, where servants immediately brought wine and food. Nebuchadnezzar watched his two military advisors, as neither man liked the other. Nebuchadnezzar's father had taught him that it was best to have men who distrusted one another as advisors. In that way, one would always be sure to receive the pros and cons of all proposals if for no other reason than each advisor would point out the flaws in the other man's arguments.

"It has been three days since the terms were delivered to the Hebrews," began Nebuchadnezzar. "Have they given you an answer?"

Naaman smiled as he looked first at Nebuchadnezzar and then at Shamgar. He clapped his hands and a servant entered. "Bring me the list," he ordered. The servant disappeared into another chamber of the tent, and emerged with a scroll and handed it to Naaman.

"This list was brought to us this morning," Naaman said as he unrolled the scroll and laid it on a table. Shamgar and Nebuchadnezzar looked over the list. The names were divided into groups describing their training and position in Hebrew society.

"When will they be ready to assemble for departure to Babylon?" asked Shamgar.

"Even as we speak, my men are gathering the exiles so that they will be ready to leave at dawn tomorrow."

"This is excellent, Naaman," Nebuchadnezzar said, a broad smile spreading across his face.

"My only concern, King Nebuchadnezzar, is that Jehoiakim will use this as an opportunity to deport his political rivals. We will have nothing but malcontents coming to Babylon." Naaman was still uncomfortable with the decision to bring these people to Babylon, and he felt it his duty to at least cover his back side in case any negative consequences arose.

"Jehoiakim will use this as an opportunity to rid himself of his critics, it is true. However, this will add to our benefit," said Shamgar, seizing the opportunity to disparage his rival. "These exiles will appreciate the opportunity to get out from under his rule. They will be eager to make a fresh start. We will groom them for positions of importance in Babylon. In time, they will come to be thankful for this day."

Nebuchadnezzar watched Naaman bristle ever so slightly at Shamgar's words. He knew that Naaman was not happy with the prospect of foreign nationals on Babylonian soil. Nebuchadnezzar was sure, however, that that opinion would change in time.

Timeline of Events
612 BC. Babylonians and Medes conquer Assyria
609 BC. King Josiah of Judah killed in battle with Egyptians. His son Jehoiakim becomes king in Judah.
605 BC. Babylonians battle Egyptians at Carchemish
605 BC. Nebuchadnezzar becomes king of Babylon
605 BC. The Babylonians invade Judah
605 BC. First wave of deportation of Jews to Babylon
605 BC. Daniel is taken captive and begins to prophesy
597 BC. Zedekiah Became King of Judah
586 BC. Jerusalem sacked and burned by the Babylonians

"Here is what we must do, then," said Nebuchadnezzar. "We will send a messenger to order that the exiles be ready to leave at dawn, along with the tribute. A battalion shall be sent to escort them back to Babylon. We shall then go to Ashkelon where we will exact tribute and deportees there. From there, we will proceed to Tyre. With the Egyptians in disarray, I plan to send Shamgar down the coast establishing outposts and filling our treasury. By this time next year, we will be ready to march against Egypt and crush her once and for all. That is my destiny, and I intend to fulfill it."

With that, the meeting was adjourned. Nebuchadnezzar emerged from Naaman's tent and made his way to his own tent which had been erected while the three of them met. Nebuchadnezzar wasn't sure which man was right about how the exiles would adapt to Babylon. He only knew that this had been his father's plan. Because of that, Nebuchadnezzar would carry it out. It would soon be dark, and he had much he needed to do in preparation for the meeting with Jehoiakim in the morning. As he traversed the remaining yards to his tent, his only wish was that he was as sure of himself as he pretended in front of his men.

Daniel looked back at his parents for what he knew would be the last time. He could see his mother crying. Beside her, his father stood straight and tall, his face displaying no emotion. But to Daniel's surprise, his father had given him something of infinite value. Once again, to reassure himself that he had it on his person, he grasped the bulge in the nap sack which hung on his back. And once again, he felt the outline of two scrolls nestled within. One was his father's copy of the Torah - the five books of the law given word for word - some said even letter by letter - to Moses by Jehovah God.

The document had been missing for over one hundred years,

hidden during the reign of the evil king Manasseh. Workers restoring a portion of the temple wall had found it only a few years before Daniel had been born. When King Josiah was yet a lad, his father had been one of the scribes assigned the task of recopying the Torah. So exacting were the requirements of making the copy - not one letter could be changed - that Daniel's father had only managed to make two copies. It was said that the Torah contained the secrets of the universe, but only those blessed by God would ever unlock its meaning. For the first time in years, Daniel realized that his father truly loved him.

He walked on, his train of thought distracted by the sight of other exiles who, like himself, were no friends of King Jehoiakim. There were Shadrach, Meshach, and Abednego, three of Daniel's friends who had helped in the rescue of Jeremiah when Jehoiakim had sought to have the prophet killed. So this is how Jehoiakim would rid himself of those who opposed him! But not all were Jehoiakim's enemies. Shemaiah, a rival of Jeremiah, was also going - no doubt to spy on Jehoiakim's foes in exile.

As they marched, Daniel could see the king of Babylon, Nebuchadnezzar, watching them leave. Beside him stood his hated right-hand man, Naaman, the Captain of the Guard. Daniel thought bitterly of the note that Ezekiel - who would be allowed to remain in Jerusalem - had slipped him. It had been written by Jeremiah, now in hiding. "Upon your shoulders God has placed the burden of His people. You are the key to returning them safely. Remember, things are not always as they may appear. You must be a father to Nebuchadnezzar. The Lord will provide a way for that to happen. May the Lord bless you and keep you."

Words! Just words! Ezekiel and Jeremiah weren't being forced to abandon their homes! Daniel cursed the day he had ever become involved with Jeremiah.

Just then, Daniel saw flying above the head of Nebuchadnezzar a large bald eagle. He watched it high above, and became mesmerized as he watched it circle. Once, twice, three times ... it circled seven times, and then flew East in the direction of Babylon. Daniel's thoughts were jerked back to the second scroll hidden in his pack - the Scroll of Isaiah. Like the Torah, it too contained wisdom and prophecy. Daniel had committed much of it to memory already. At the sight of the eagle, those words came rushing at him now:

"Those who wait upon the Lord will renew their strength. They shall rise up with wings as eagles. They shall run and not be weary. They shall walk and not faint."

With those words, all the bitterness flowed out of him. Just as quickly, he felt an abiding peace. He thought of Jeremiah's message. Mere words? No. Daniel realized that they were much more than mere words - God did have some great purpose in store for him. Daniel set his mind to the task at hand, and settled into a steady pace. It would be a long march.

CHAPTER 6

Nebuchadnezzar Returns to Babylon

So, King Nebuchadnezzar has returned," Haman said to an empty balcony as he watched the army approach the gates of Babylon. As the Chief Priest in the court of first Nabopolassar and now Nebuchadnezzar, Haman wielded immense power. He controlled all of the temple estates, as well as the revenues generated by the sale of goods produced on them. Haman also collected the taxes levied on those goods, and kept a percentage of the levies before passing them on to the civil authorities. As Chief Priest, Haman was responsible for the spiritual well being of the kingdom, while the King was responsible for protecting the land and expanding the reach of the kingdom. But now, Haman wanted absolute power, and he had devised a plan to attain it.

Haman's chambers lay in the temple of Esagila, "the building which is the Foundation of Heaven and Earth." Haman's chambers were near the top of the temple, which had a commanding view of the terrain as far as the eye could see. Descending to the ground level of the edifice, he climbed into a carriage that awaited to take him to the city gates where he would greet Nebuchadnezzar. Haman had prepared a banquet to honor the king. Some of the finest Hebrew youth would be on display for Nebuchadnezzar's review.

Crowds were now gathering on either side of the road leading to the Ishtar Gate where Nebuchadnezzar would enter. Haman's carriage began to traverse the Bridge of the Heavens, which spanned the

Euphrates River. Long ago, the architects of Babylon had conceived of a city, wholly self-contained and impervious to attack. They had built the city around a stretch of the Euphrates river, which flowed under the walls on the south and north ends of the city. If anyone ever attempted to lay siege, her inhabitants would be insured a source of fresh water, as well as fish to eat.

The inner two walls of the city were twenty feet high and separated by a space of twenty-four feet. This space was filled with compacted dirt upon which a road had been constructed so that two chariots could ride side by side around the city. Nine city gates, named after the gods of the Babylonians, guarded the entrances to the city. These gates opened out onto bridges that spanned a canal which circled the city. A quarter-league from this wall, a similar outer wall circled the city. If any invaders were to breach the outer wall, they would be demoralized by facing an even more daunting assault against the ramparts of the inner wall. It was truly a city conceived by the gods themselves.

Haman's carriage came to the mouth of the Ishtar Gate. The dragons and bulls engraved on the gate's surface seemingly came alive as the sunlight reflected off the glazed finish of the edifice. Already, the drawbridge was being lowered to span the fifty-foot moat that surrounded the wall. Nebuchadnezzar, along with Naaman's palace guard and their captives, drew near. Haman mounted the platform that had been prepared, and gave the signal for the trumpets to sound. Along the walls of the city, more citizens had appeared to greet their king.

"Hail Nebuchadnezzar, King of Babylon, Servant of Marduk. Your people salute you. And hail Naaman, Captain of the Palace Guard." Haman raised his arms as he greeted Nebuchadnezzar and Naaman. On cue, the crowds began to roar their approval. Banners showing King Nebuchadnezzar seated on his throne, the sun and moon looking down over his shoulders, were unfurled. Nebuchadnezzar rode in waving to his people.

Behind him came the exiles that were being brought into the city. They had been marching for the last two months, ever since they left with the Hebrews from Jerusalem. But there were many other exile groups: Philistines from Ashkelon. Edomites from Petra. All the various peoples which Nebuchadnezzar was bringing to Babylon held an ancient and abiding hatred for one another. More specifically, these people hated the Hebrews. Haman smiled inwardly as he thought about them, with their fanatical religion. What fools! The Hebrews were an arrogant people who alone among the nations claimed that there was only one God - their God. They would tolerate no other. It was because of their intolerance and claim that they among all the people of the earth served the one and only true God, that they were held in contempt by the rest of the world.

Haman was counting on that hatred to kindle a fire that would consume Nebuchadnezzar. When it did, he would step in to fill the void. He would magnanimously allow the exiles to return to their homes. He would then inherit the empire Nebuchadnezzar was building, and have allies in the different kingdoms controlled by Babylon loyal to him.

WAIT A MINUTE, GRANDPA!

Mouth wide open, Grandpa stopped talking and looked down at Nadia.

"She's been trying to get your attention for the last minute, Grandpa!" said a clearly exasperated Nai Nai to her husband. "Take a break and let Nadia ask her question."

"Ah, sorry, Nadia. What is your question?" asked a sheepish Grandpa as he took off his fake beard and mustache.

"Grandpa, I never heard of these other people - the Edomites, the

Ashkelonites – all those Ites! Who were they? Were they friends of Daniel's people?"

"Great question, Nadia. Here, let me explain with the use of this map." Grandpa pulled out a yard stick to point with and walked over to a map.

"Now," began Grandpa, "Jerusalem was here in what was called the Country of Judah. Ever since the time of Moses, there were different groups of people who hated the Jews because after they left Egypt, they came to the land of Canaan, the land God gave them. When they got there, they fought many battles with the tribes who lived there. Those tribes were all the 'ites' I've been talking about. For over a thousand years, they stayed mad, and looked for a way to get revenge."

As Grandpa pointed to different places – Ammon, Moab, Edom – he told them the history of how the nations came to be, and why they didn't like the Jews. Pointing to a city near the coast of the Mediterranean Sea called Ashkelon, he said: "Ashkelon was one of the last cities of the Philistines. They worshipped a god called Dagon. The people of Ashkelon would do terrible things in the worship of their god. This was another reason why the Jews and these different tribes hated each other."

Nadia was still determined to get her questions answered. "But Grandpa, if these people didn't like the Jews, and Babylon was taking some of their people and bringing them to live in Babylon just like Daniel and his people, wouldn't they cause problems?"

"What kind of problems do you mean, Nadia?" asked Isaiah.

"Well, some of the kids from school all came to America from a

---

The Canaanite Gods

Who were the gods Chemosh, Dagon, Molech – the gods of the Canaanites?

For the most part, they were the same god, but with a different name depending on where they were worshipped. They were worshipped in the countries of Amon, Ashkelon, Edom and Moab.

Sometimes, their worshippers offered human sacrifices burned in a fire when worshiping their gods.

different country. They speak a different language. The teachers work really hard to have everyone get along, but sometimes there are fights in the restrooms. So, I figure if that sort of thing happens at my school now, then maybe it happened back in the time of Daniel, too."

"Excellent question, Nadia! What do you think about that, Grandpa?" asked Nai Nai with one of her sternest grandmotherly looks.

"I have to go to the bathroom," announced Josiah matter-of-factly as he got up and left the room. At that point, everyone stopped talking for a few seconds while Josiah left the room. Then, everyone broke out laughing.

"Nadia," said Grandpa after catching his breath, "You raise a very good question. You're right, the same sort of hatred and fighting would probably have happened between the different exile groups in Babylon. Tell you what. Let's all take a short bathroom break, and then I'll resume the story. I promise to tell you something that answers the very thing you are asking about, Nadia. Deal?"

Nadia nodded his head. "Deal, Grandpa."

CHAPTER 7

Daniel Meets King Nebuchadnezzar

ABOUT TEN MINUTES later, the children returned to the sunroom, having finished their break. Nai Nai served fresh popcorn. With everyone settled back in their seats, Grandpa put his costume back on, turned to the next page of The Chronicles of Belteshazzar, and resumed his story.

And so the Lion of Babylon vanquished the Bull at Carchemish. In that same year, he carried off to the Land of Shinar the vessels of the Temple of Solomon. To her gates, he brought not only the chosen ones of Zion. Nebuchadnezzar also brought captives of other nations, including Philistines from the City of Ashkelon. The days passed quickly in our new home in the Land of Shinar. Their king, Nebuchadnezzar, took a special interest in the training of my friends and I. This is the tale of how I was chosen to become one of the Wise Men, a Mage of Babylon.

The Chronicles of Belteshazzar

"Tell me, Potiphar, how have your Israelite pupils been doing?" asked King Nebuchadnezzar. Ever since returning from his battles against the Egyptians at Carchemish and bringing the captives of several conquered people back to Babylon, he had been too busy with the politics of his Court to see what was happening with the training of his most promising exiles.

"In the three months that they have been in my charge, they have excelled, oh king. I have invited several of them to join us this evening. They are sitting over there." Potiphar pointed to a group of Hebrews, among whom were Daniel and his friends, Shadrack, Meshack and Abednego.

Nebuchadnezzar looked in the direction Potiphar, his servant in charge of training the Hebrews, indicated. "They are not eating and drinking. Why is that?"

"Oh, my King, they have told us their God forbids them to eat the food we serve them. They do not seem to suffer for it, so I have not made an issue of it."

Nebuchadnezzar scratched his beard for a moment, and then drained his cup of wine. "Nonsense! I want them trained in all our ways - <u>all</u>! They must be strong and healthy to do so. They must become like us. Henceforth, you shall require them to eat our food, or I will have your head! Is that understood?"

"Yes, oh king. Beginning tomorrow, it shall be done."

"You heard Nebuchadnezzar! If you do not eat the food prepared by my people, I will lose my head!" Potiphar said emphatically to the brash young man before him.

Daniel and his three closest friends had known their decision would not be easy. But, Potiphar had to be made to understand that they could not compromise on this point.

"Potiphar, you have been kind and just to us since the day we arrived here. Meshach, Shadrach, Abednego and I have prospered under your instruction. The goal of both of us is that my friends and I be able to serve Babylon to the best of our abilities. Would you not agree with that?"

Potiphar looked at his pupil impatiently. "Yes, yes of course. What is your point?"

"We believe that we can best do this by eating the foods prescribed by our religion. You believe that Babylonian food is best for us. Therefore, let us test this. For the next ten days, the four of us will eat only our kind of food. All the other Israelite youths will eat Babylonian food. If, at the end of ten days, our appearance does not surpass that of the others, we will eat the Babylonian food. However, if our appearance surpasses that of the others, we will continue to eat our food. Agreed?"

Potiphar looked at Daniel, his brows furled. "I don't know why, but I will do as you ask. For both our sakes, don't disappoint me."

It was the day they had waited for, and Daniel and his friends were ready. How quickly most of the Hebrew exiles had taken to the lifestyle of their Babylonian "hosts." Most of Daniel's contemporaries ate pork, as well as meat sacrificed to the Babylonian idols. He was disgusted by his countrymen's willingness to compromise on their beliefs. Today was the day for Nebuchadnezzar to render his judgment. Without intending it, Daniel had made sure that he and his friends would come to the attention of the King of Babylon.

"Daniel, quit day dreaming and get a move on," Abednego said from the doorway of Daniel's room. "We must assemble in the courtyard, and you're running late as usual."

Daniel stood up and made sure his tunic and cloak were in proper order. "You're always in a rush. Relax, Abednego!" Daniel teased, grinning at his friend. He sauntered slowly over in Abednego's direction, and then with a quick twist of his body, moved past him and out the door. As he did so, Daniel called out, "Come on, let's go, or we'll be late!"

They descended the stairs that led from the second floor balcony of their quarters into the enclosed courtyard below. Most of the other Hebrew pupils in Potiphar's charge were already there. A few other stragglers besides Daniel and Abednego came from other parts of the oval compound surrounding the courtyard. They fell into line and began to march toward the reviewing area.

Their Babylonian masters awaited them, conferring among themselves. "Thus it begins," Nebuchadnezzar said to Naaman and Haman on either side of him. "Babylon will become a melting pot. We will train these different peoples, who will then be ambassadors for us to their own people. No other empire in all history has attempted what we are doing. They have all made the fatal mistake of attempting to enslave the people they have conquered. In the end, the desire for freedom has led to the ultimate overthrow of the conqueror."

Neither man, not knowing the thoughts of the other, wished to challenge Nebuchadnezzar on this point of philosophy. Instead, they turned their attention to Potiphar as he led his charges to assemble in front of them.

Nebuchadnezzar walked down the steps of the review platform so that he could inspect the Hebrew youths. He spent several minutes walking among them, until he came to Daniel, Shadrach, Meshach and Abednego. He paused in front of them and eyed them closely. "Potiphar, these four appear to be stronger and more healthy than the rest." He looked at the four of them. All but Daniel's eyes were averted, gazing at the dirt beneath their feet. "To what do you attribute this?" he asked looking directly into Daniel's eyes.

The moment of truth. Daniel had to choose between telling the truth or telling a lie. They were supposed to have been eating the Babylonian food. If Nebuchadnezzar found out they hadn't, they were dead. Yet Daniel couldn't lie! Carefully, he spoke the words he had rehearsed for just this moment.

"Does my lord the king always seek to do the will of Marduk?" Daniel asked.

"Yes. My duty is to serve the God of the Earth. Why do you ask?"

"Like you, I seek to serve my God. But I have also been taught to obey the orders of my king. How could I do both?" Daniel asked.

He watched the expression on Nebuchadnezzar's face change to a frown. Daniel spoke quickly. "I convinced my friends that we should eat only the food ordered by our God for ten days. After that time, if the food of our God caused us to find favor in your sight, we would have pleased you. If the food of our God did not cause us to find favor, we would then eat the food prepared in the Babylonian way. The food of Marduk would have been proven superior to the food of our God, and you would have been honored. In this way, I have pleased both my God and my king."

Daniel looked into Nebuchadnezzar's eyes. The king was only seven years older than he. Daniel did not know what he would do.

"Hiii! I like this one!" Nebuchadnezzar shouted, a smile engulfing his face, looking at those around him. "Other men are afraid to speak plainly to me. My wise men are more concerned about being patronizing than being wise. It is refreshing to find a man like this one, wise before he is old." Nebuchadnezzar turned his gaze back to Daniel. "What is your name?"

"Daniel, my king."

"Haman! From this day forward, he is to be an apprentice in your care. He shall enter into the service of my Magi. I will have him as one of my wise men."

> **The Gods of Babylon**
>
> **Enki** was a Babylonian god of water who was the father of the chief god Marduk
>
> **Ishtar** was a Babylonian goddess, the wife of Enki and the mother of Marduk.
>
> **Marduk** the storm god was the chief god of the Babylonians who slew Tiamat.
>
> **Tiamat** was the Babylonian goddess of the oceans whom the other Babylonian gods sought to destroy.

Haman looked at Daniel and back at Nebuchadnezzar. "It shall be as you command." He bowed quickly to hide his face, flushed with anger and embarrassment. A Hebrew elevated to the court of Babylon? Marduk forbid it!

CHAPTER 8

The Babylonian Captain of the Guard

THE TENSION IN the air was increasing, and as the man responsible for protecting the king, Naaman didn't like it. As he had expected, the Hebrews and the Ashkelonites weren't getting along - his men had already had to break up several fights. Other groups like the Moabites and the Ammonites were involved too, but the first two groups were the worst. The tension between the Hebrews and Ashkelonites was spilling over into the general population, causing the people of Babylon to criticize Nebuchadnezzar's war against Egypt.

Frustrated and in need of release from the stress he was feeling, Naaman decided to go for a walk. Not one to walk leisurely, he strode with purpose through the crowded streets. Naaman paid little attention to the shopkeepers peddling their wares. Because no one wanted to draw the attention of an armed soldier, Naaman's introspection was not disturbed.

He came to the Temple of Ishtar, the mother of Marduk and the goddess of love and war. While he didn't pay a lot of attention to the official religion of his people, he certainly respected those who did. He noted that they were preparing for the feast that would be held at the end of the week to celebrate the coming of spring, and the new year.

As he rounded a corner of the temple, Naaman saw something

that absolutely astounded him. He was on the walkway surrounding the temple. In the courtyard below him, he saw an Israelite beating a man from Ashkelon. A small crowd began to gather around the fight when another man burst through the crowd to pull the Israelite off his victim. His cloak had the markings of the Wise Men's office - it was the new advisor to Nebuchadnezzar - what was his name? Daniel! And a Hebrew! Naaman looked quickly for the stairwell that would lead down to the courtyard and, finding it, descended several steps at a time.

"That is enough! All of you, leave now!" Naaman roared, drawing his sword. The small crowd and the original Hebrew combatant fled at the sight of Naaman. Daniel went over to the Ashkelon man, who lay on the ground rubbing his sore head.

"Thank you for coming when you did," Daniel said to Naaman as he examined the bruise on the man's head. He made sure that the man was all right, then rose to face the Captain of the Imperial Guard.

"I saw what you did," Naaman said. "It was extraordinary. Why would you risk helping an Ashkelonite against one of your own people?"

"For the simple reason that the attack on that poor man was unprovoked. What would you expect me to do?"

"I would expect you to stay out of it, at a minimum!" Naaman retorted before he realized what he was doing. More softly, he continued, "I have not seen anyone like you. You defy the King's commandments, and he rewards you by making you a magi. You come across a fellow countryman beating a sworn enemy, and you side with the sworn enemy. I would enjoy learning more about what motivates you to act the way you do."

"For my part, I would value learning more about the people of the King I am to serve. Shall we get something to eat? I'm hungry."

"Of course, we have laws against murder and stealing. But no law would cause a Chaldean to side against his own kindred. What you did today is unthinkable to the Babylonian mind." Naaman was exasperated by his dinner guest. They had finished their meal and now sat and talked, sipping their wine.

Daniel sighed. "Let me try to explain this a different way. We met outside the Temple of Ishtar, the Mother of Marduk. Yet Marduk is your chief god - greater than his mother and father, Enki. I have heard a little of how this came to be, but before I make my point, explain your religion to me in your own words. How did Marduk come to be your chief god?"

Naaman took a gulp of his wine and cleared his throat. "The great oceans rose up to consume the earth. The goddess of the ocean, Tiamat, would not listen to reason, and so the rest of the gods set out to destroy her. One after another, Tiamat killed those that came against her. Then Marduk made a deal with the Council of Gods. He would destroy Tiamat if they would make him king of the gods. They agreed, and he succeeded in killing her, along with her lieutenant, Kingu. At the suggestion of his father, Enki, Marduk made man from the blood of Kingu."

Daniel took a long drought from his wine goblet and looked into the pool of dark liquid. Without looking up, he said, "What is the purpose of man, then? What happened next?"

"Until man was created, the gods had worked to grow crops and feed themselves. After Marduk created man, the gods treated man as their slave. As man multiplied, a great deal of noise was made here on earth, so the gods decided to send a flood to destroy him. Enki, however, warned a man named Utnapishtim, who built a large boat so that his family and many animals would survive the flood. When the flood came, it lasted seven days. After the flood ended and the boat landed on dry ground, Utnapishtim offered sacrifice to Enki and to Marduk. The gods, so hungry were they because they had not eaten, flocked around his sacrifice like flies and consumed it. Because they realized that they needed man to feed them, they decided never again to destroy mankind."

Daniel leaned forward, and looked into Naaman's eyes. "We have a similar story of how a flood came upon mankind, but there are a few key differences," said Daniel. "Would you like to hear them?"

"Yes," said Naaman. "But I'm not sure how this ties into the explanation of why you would help an alien against your own kindred."

"You will see in a moment," replied Daniel. "Like you, we have a flood story. It involves a man called Noah who, like Utnapishtim, was told to build a great ark. Noah thus saved both his family and two of every living creature. It rained for forty days and forty nights, after which Noah and his family floated in the boat for a long time before finally landing on dry ground."

"But that is where the similarity ends. We believe in one God, while you believe in many. God caused the flood, not because man was making 'too much noise,' but because man had committed many evil sins. Men were not only sinning against God, they were sinning against each other. When Noah's ark finally found land he offered a sacrifice to God. God promised never to destroy man again by a flood, but not because He needed man to feed Him. No. God made that promise because He loves all men. Your gods want you to serve them; to be their slaves. Our God wants us to love Him, and know Him as both Lord and friend. Our God wants us to live just, moral lives, treating all men equally."

"And that is why you helped the Ashkelon man? Because your god wants you to treat all men equally?" asked Naaman.

"Yes," said Daniel.

"Then your god is a weak god. I have watched your two peoples interact. You are the first Israelite I have seen act the way you did. If your god wants you to treat all men equally, then he can't be a strong god - no one except you obeys him!"

Daniel eyed his host. Naaman was visibly agitated over this

conversation. Instead of exhibiting confidence and self-superiority in his derision of Daniel, he seemed to be struggling over some inner turmoil.

"What if I told you that before you came to Jerusalem, even before you defeated Egypt at Carchemish, one of our wise men - a prophet named Jeremiah - prophesied what would happen to my country of Judah?"

"What!?"

"You heard me. Not only did he foretell that this would happen, but that it was our God's will that we be taken into captivity by Nebuchadnezzar. And, he foretold how long we shall be in captivity in Babylon."

Naaman was dumbfounded. "How long?" he said meekly.

"For seventy years."

"Why on earth would your god want Nebuchadnezzar to defeat you - to see our god Marduk triumph over him?"

"So that we would be punished for our sins. So that we would eventually repent, and be returned to our land, and give our God the glory for having done so."

Naaman looked at his wine goblet and mulled over what Daniel had said. What this Hebrew said made absolutely no sense. He drained the contents of his goblet, slamming it down on the table.

"I have told Nebuchadnezzar that this idea of his, bringing people from different cultures together here in Babylon, is a mistake. Already, tensions mount between your peoples. Our people are beginning to complain about what is happening. They question sending our armies to Palestine and our plans to invade Egypt. Are you a spy?"

"I am sworn to serve Nebuchadnezzar. No, Naaman, I am not a spy."

At that moment, a knock came at the door. Naaman rose to speak with the person there. After a few minutes, the messenger left and Naaman walked back to the middle of the room. He stood there with his arms folded, looking at Daniel.

"I have orders to report to the palace at the command of King Nebuchadnezzar. This will be our last planning meeting to review plans to send our army to invade Egypt. I will be gone for a long time – perhaps a year. If you are committed to serving Nebuchadnezzar, know that there are those in his court who would serve him ill."

Daniel rose to take his leave. "I will pray that you return safely, and soon. When do you leave?"

"In three days. Now, you must go. I have much to do."

"Until we meet again." Daniel bowed his head and left. Naaman sat for a moment, thinking of what had just transpired. To him, religion was for the weak minded, but he had never met anyone like Daniel. The Israelite was certainly not weak minded. Naaman could not think of another holy man who took his religion as seriously as did this Daniel.

CHAPTER 9

Grandpa Answers Nadia's Question

G RANDPA, DID THAT really happen? Did Daniel and Naaman actually have that conversation?" Nadia looked up at her grandfather, expectantly waiting for an answer.

"Nadia, we don't have anything that says that a conversation like the one I just told you a story about took place. But we do know that the Babylonians had their own story of how the flood happened. We know about all the Babylonian Gods, and how they believed the world came into existence. Now, if Daniel and the Captain of the Babylonian Guard were real people – and I certainly believe they were – doesn't it make sense that they would have talked about things like their religious beliefs?" Grandpa stopped and looked at all three children as he waited for them to answer.

Finally, Isaiah spoke up. "Tonight at dinner, you asked me how I was doing at school and I told you I got an A on a history test, and a B+ on a math test. And, I told you that I tried out for the soccer team. But, I didn't tell you EVERYTHING I did, or about EVERY conversation I had with my friends. But, even if I don't tell you about every single thing I did during the week, you could imagine some of those things and sort of tell a story about them as though they did happen. Right, Grandpa?"

"Yes, Isaiah. In fact, I might say that you played chess with your friend Phil, and that he beat you. And, because he beat you, you decided to go to the library to check out a book on how to play chess better. Now, Isaiah, I don't know if that happened or not, but since you like to play chess, and you have a friend named Phil, is what I just said something that you can see yourself actually doing?"

"Wow, Grandpa. Something like that DID sort of happen. My friend Eric beat me yesterday. I asked him how he got so good at chess, and he showed me a chess book he got from the library. I decided that the next time I was there, I'd try to find a book on how to play chess better."

Turning to Nadia, Grandpa said, "You see Nadia, your idea that there would have been fights among all the different people exiled to Babylon is a very reasonable idea. It's reasonable because you know what people do today when they are around other people who aren't like them. And, even though I didn't know anything about Isaiah's conversation with his friend Eric, I could imagine something like that story because we all know that Isaiah likes to play chess – and that he hates losing!"

Grandpa walked over to his computer and turned it on. After a few moments, he googled a TV show called Babylon 5. Once he had it on the screen, he played a short video about the show. Here's what the trailer's narrator said:

It was the dawn of the third age of mankind 10 years after the earth-minbari war. The Babylon project was a dream given form. Its goal: To prevent another war by creating a place where humans and aliens could work out their differences peacefully. It's a port of call, a home away from home for diplomats, hustlers, entrepreneurs, and wanderers. Humans and aliens wrapped in 2,500,000 tons of spinning metal, all alone in the night. It can be a dangerous place but it's our last best hope for peace. This is the story of the last of the Babylon stations. The year is 2258. The name of the place is Babylon 5.

"Kids, the TV show Babylon 5 came on the Sci Fi channel in 1994, back when your dad was about your age. It was a place where representatives from different alien planets came to discuss their differences and have a way of keeping peace between a lot of people who had a history of fighting each other. Now, what if Daniel, or someone like him, were to create a council where representatives of the different tribes could meet and work out their differences?"

"Just like they did in the show Babylon 5, Grandpa?" asked Josiah.

"Yes, Josiah. Just like in that TV show." Grandpa smiled at his grandchildren. "We'll never know if anything like that happened. In Chapter 2 of Daniel, the Captain of the Babylonian Guard goes looking for Daniel and his friends. His orders are to kill them. Now, if the King of Babylon has given his soldiers orders to kill somebody, what do you think King Nebuchadnezzar would do to any soldier who didn't carry out his orders?"

"Off with his head!" Cried Isaiah excitedly.

"Exactly!" Replied Grandpa. But guess what happened?

The kids all shrugged their shoulders. Grandpa looked at them for a long moment, and then said; "Instead of killing Daniel when he found him, the Babylonian Captain of the guard had a conversation with Daniel, told him what was going on, and Daniel asked that he be taken to see King Nebuchadnezzar and talk to him." Grandpa got up, turned off his computer, and turned back to look at his grandchildren.

"I thought for a long time and asked myself why the Captain of the Guard didn't just kill Daniel there and then. There is only one answer I could come up with as to why Daniel was spared. Do you know what I decided?"

"That God didn't want him to die." replied Josiah.

"Yes, Josiah, God didn't want Daniel to die! And because of that, there must have been situations where Daniel had opportunities to speak with that man. That they became friends. And when the time came to carry out King Nebuchadnezzar's order kill Daniel, he couldn't because they were already friends. I think God created a set of circumstances that allowed Daniel and the Captain of the Guard to become friends, so when the order came to kill Daniel, they talked about the situation, because that's what friends do."

Nadia thought for a moment, and then, as though a light bulb had just turned on in her head, Nadia said: "So, Grandpa, your story about Daniel and Naaman talking about their different flood stories and their religions is an example of how you imagine the two of them getting to know each other and become friends. Right?"

"Right, Nadia! Now, let's get back to the story!"

CHAPTER 10

Daniel Proposes a Council of Exiles

Having changed back into his costume, Grandpa re-entered the Sunroom. "You know, Nadia brought up a great point – Daniel made friends with the Captain of the Babylonian Guard; a man who could help him earn the trust of King Nebuchadnezzar. As you listen to the story, think about how Daniel's friendship with Naaman led to a way to solve a problem that Nebuchadnezzar faced. From this story, we learn that there is always a reason God brings people into our lives." With that as an introduction, Grandpa turned the page in The Chronicles of Belteshazzar, and resumed the story.

In the seventh year of King Jehoiakim, Pharaoh Necho defeated Nebuchadnezzar. Thus, for a time, the Lion of the East was silenced, and so the pride of Jehoiakim's heart led him to rebel against Babylon. The Lord used the events at Migdol to stiffen the neck of Jehoiakim, and thereby cause his downfall. Thus the King of Judah consorted with the agents of evil to assassinate The Lord's anointed, and failed.

The Chronicles of Belteshazzar

Naaman rubbed the spot on his neck where, four months ago, he had been injured when Babylon had fought a major battle with Egypt at a place called Migdol. They had been winning until an army of Greek mercenaries arrived and joined the Egyptian army against the Babylonians. The battle had lasted for several days. Naaman himself had been gravely wounded. He had been out for several days, and so did not remember how the Babylonian army had retreated. He knew that he was lucky to be alive.

Nebuchadnezzar's army had made it back to Babylon from Migdol only a week and a half ago. They had returned to find the nation of Elam to their south stirring up trouble. The strife between the exile communities and the native Chaldeans was also intensifying. This was a dangerous time for Babylon, and the strain was beginning to show on Nebuchadnezzar.

And then had come a bit of news this morning that might shed a ray of hope on the situation. The war council had received a report that Pharaoh Necho was dead of a heart attack, and that his son, Hophra, had succeeded him to the throne. Additionally, it had been learned that king Anlaman of Kush was intending to regain territory lost to Egypt nearly sixty years ago. As Naaman examined a map of Egypt's Southern frontier, his mind turned over the plans that had been made.

Even now, an envoy was preparing to leave for Kush and convey the support of Nebuchadnezzar to King Anlaman. While soldiers were not being sent, this year's tribute from the conquered nations of Palestine would be sent directly to Kush. Nebuchadnezzar wanted that nation's help to open a prolonged two-front war against Egypt. If Babylon were ever again to launch an attack against Egypt, she would need the help of Kush to prevent Egypt's southern army from joining the fight as they had at Migdol.

So intent had Naaman's thoughts

> **Egypt Builds a Canal**
>
> Around 600 B.C., Pharaoh Necho "conceived the notion of canalizing the Wadi Tumilat by cutting a waterway, 'the canal of the east'. (Source: _Egypt, Canaan, and Israel in Ancient Times_).
>
> Babylon attacked Egypt near this canal in 601 B.C. at a place called Migdol.

been as he studied the map that he had failed to hear the knock at the door. One of his guards had opened it, and clearing his throat, announced "The Magi Daniel wishes to speak with you."

Naaman stood to his full height, but without turning replied, "Send him in."

Daniel entered the room, and Naaman beckoned him over to the map. "This, Daniel, is the expanse of Nebuchadnezzar's empire. For the past decade, relations with Elam to our south have been quiet, allowing us to concentrate on subduing the Assyrians and extending our reach to the border of Egypt. We were defeated here, at Migdol, earlier this year. Egypt is building a canal there so that their navy can sail from the Mediterranean Sea through to the Red Sea. From there, they can sail around the Arabian peninsula and up the Euphrates river to attack Babylon."

Naaman traced the points on the map as he discussed them. Concluding his explanation, he turned to Daniel and said: "But our destiny will not long be denied. How does it feel to serve in the court of one who will someday rule the world?"

"I serve where my God chooses for me to serve, Naaman," Daniel responded. "And it is my duty to Nebuchadnezzar that has brought me to see you, for unless he is able to rule his capitol, he will lose his kingdom."

Naaman knew that Daniel, though a foreigner, desired nothing but to serve Nebuchadnezzar honorably. He admired this young man, wise beyond his years, and thought back to when he first spoke with him after Daniel had rescued the Ashkelonite from his fellow Hebrews. He would listen to what Daniel had to say. He turned to face Daniel. "You and I have spoken of this before. It is too late to undo the course we are on, bringing exiles like yourself to be assimilated into our culture. What is it that brings you here?"

"Over the past few months, two ideas have emerged as to how to reduce the tension in the city," Daniel began. "One course, championed by Haman and the one we are currently pursuing, calls for patrols of soldiers to crack down on disturbances. These patrols have become increasingly violent in their approach. Furthermore, your soldiers have begun to conduct spot searches of the exiles' homes whenever they see fit. More often than not, these searches are triggered by informants whose reports of illegal activity are made up stories. In reality, they use your soldiers so they can have their rivals arrested, or cause trouble for competing exile groups. In either case, the result is that this policy is increasing, not decreasing, the hatred of the exile groups for each other, as well as the Babylonians authorities."

"And the other course of action which, I assume, you want my help in supporting, is - what?" asked Naaman.

"I believe a council made up of representatives of the exile groups needs to be formed. This council would meet to resolve tensions peaceably. Furthermore, I believe that the patrols, instead of responding only when fights or other provocations occur, should attempt to build positive relations. By working with the communities they police, they will get to know the people there. This way, the level of violence will be reduced, and we will truly begin to build ties of cooperation instead of hatred."

Naaman took a long look at Daniel, and blinked. Twice. In the moments between the closing and opening of his eyelids the first and second times, Naaman "saw" a concept which was totally foreign to him. Throughout his life, the use of force was the first, nay, the only option, he had ever really considered to resolve conflict. Naaman never avoided a fight. He welcomed it, and applied the use of superior force to overpower his opponent. Subjugation, not cooperation, was to be sought through the threat of force levied against any and all opponents.

Nebuchadnezzar's plan to assimilate the peoples he conquered rested on the same principle. Force the defeated people to accept the Babylonian way of doing things, or perish. Daniel's approach would not impose decisions on the exiles: It would give them a voice in making decisions that concerned them. Naaman marveled at how differently this Hebrew thought about problems. As differently as ... as differently as how the two viewed the relationship between themselves and their respective gods.

"If we were to do as you suggest, we would appear weak in the eyes of the exiles we have brought here to serve us," Naaman countered halfheartedly.

"And by following your present course, appearing to be strong, you would in fact grow weaker as chaos mounts," Daniel shot back. "The use of violence is the first resort of the powerless. By doing as I suggest, you demonstrate confidence in your power. In so doing, you will be strengthened, not weakened."

Naaman paced around the room, not sure what to do. "So what do you want me to do?" he asked finally.

Daniel stood and spread his arms. "The patrols report to you. Select a few areas of the city to test my idea. Try it for the next thirty days, and if afterwards you believe the approach is working, tell Nebuchadnezzar and work to implement this strategy throughout Babylon."

Naaman shrugged his shoulders. "Daniel, I don't know why I'm going to do as you suggest, but I will. I am a soldier, and not concerned with politics at court. I will have two patrol sergeants speak with you in the morning so that you can give them more details on what you want them to do. But I warn you, Haman will not favor this policy. Sooner or later, he will learn of what you desire. It will not go well between you and he, so you must watch your steps."

Daniel nodded his head. "I am well aware of that, Naaman, and assure you that I will heed your warning. In the end, however, I am sure he will see the logic of what I propose. Now, if you will excuse me, I have other duties that beckon," and excused himself from Naaman's quarters.

"May your god protect you, my naive 'wise man,' " Naaman said softly to himself. In the Court of Babylon, no one played palace politics better than Haman.

CHAPTER 11

The Magi Must Die!

NEBUCHADNEZZAR AWOKE IN a cold sweat. He had dreamed dreams before, but never one so vivid. Never so, so real! It was as though he stood above his kingdom and looked down on it. Saw his kingdom as it was today and - could it be possible - how it would appear in the future. This was too great to fathom! "Guard!" Nebuchadnezzar cried out. "Guard, by Marduk, Guard!"

Two soldiers appeared at his door. "Your command, my Lord," the first of the two responded.

Nebuchadnezzar wasn't sure what his command should be. He gazed in their direction, seeing his dream instead of the two soldiers as they fidgeted. Then, snapping out of his trance-like state, he ordered: "Gather my Magi to me! Now! It is time they truly earned their keep."

"At once!" The two saluted and left. Nebuchadnezzar drew his cloak tightly about himself, staring at the wall, awaiting their arrival.

Nearly two hours had passed since Nebuchadnezzar had ordered his guards to gather his Magi in the meeting hall. Nebuchadnezzar was seated on his throne, clearly upset. He had also been drinking, though did not appear overly drunk. Naaman had never seen him so agitated and not in control of himself. As he looked around at those that were gathered there, he saw that some were missing, including Daniel. This was not good - but it could not be helped. Only Haman appeared to be at ease.

Nebuchadnezzar stood and addressed those who had gathered. "No one is to discuss this meeting beyond these walls. No one! I've called you here because I have had a dream, and it frightens me. I want you to explain it."

Two of the court magicians spoke up. "Oh King Nebuchadnezzar, live forever! Tell us your dream, and we will declare its meaning to you."

Nebuchadnezzar, his eyes red from lack of sleep and too much wine, stared them into silence, saying: "I'm not going to tell you my dream. You will tell me what it was I dreamed AND declare its meaning to me. In return, I will reward you beyond your wildest imaginations."

Naaman's eyes shifted to Haman, who stood silently beside Nebuchadnezzar. Thinking back to when he entered the room, Naaman remembered that Haman had been the first to arrive - had he spoken with Nebuchadnezzar? Had he somehow convinced the King to take this brash stance on the interpretation of his dream? Naaman was sure Haman had some plan. Another of the wise men spoke up.

"But great King, what you ask is impossible. Tell us your dream and we will declare its meaning to you."

Nebuchadnezzar took several steps in the direction of the one who had spoken until he was right in front of the cowering Magi. Jabbing his finger into the chest of his magician, he said, "You are trying to buy time. You have conspired against me, chosen to lie to me. I command you, tell me the dream and declare it to me! Now!"

A fourth magician stepped forward and pleadingly said, "What you ask is impossible. No one could do this thing you ask but a god."

"Naaman!" Nebuchadnezzar roared, pointing to the four wise men who had spoken out. "Seize these four. Take them and put them in the pit. Then go and find those who are not here. When they have all been found, I want all of my Magi put to death." He looked briefly at Haman, then turned to stalk out of the room, leaving everyone except the Chief Priest anxious and in a panic.

As the guards restrained the four who had been foolish enough to speak out, Naaman saw Haman's plan. He would use this opportunity to have Daniel killed. Somehow, he would get Nebuchadnezzar to divulge the dream and then declare its meaning. Naaman knew that he must find Daniel before his guards did, and he had a good idea of where to look.

Naaman pounded on the door to the apartment of Daniel's friends. "Open in the name of King Nebuchadnezzar, or by the gods, I'll break it down!" Naaman shouted. Just as he was preparing to have his guards break down the door, it swung open to reveal Daniel and his three friends.

Pointing his sword at Daniel, Naaman said "You are to come with me. Nebuchadnezzar has commanded that you and the other Magi be put to death." He looked at the young Hebrew, who just stood there. "Get a move on, or I will drag you there myself!"

"I will come with you, Naaman, but please, there is no need for this," Daniel finally responded. "What has happened - why are you so agitated?"

Naaman spoke as they rode in his chariot back to the palace, leaving Abednego, Meshach and Shadrach in their quarters. "Nebuchadnezzar has had a dream and has demanded that his Magi not only declare its meaning, but describe the dream's contents as well. When they could not do this, Nebuchadnezzar commanded that all the Magi be put to death, including those who weren't there, like yourself." Naaman didn't want to add that he believed Haman had somehow found a way to use this circumstance to get rid of Daniel. Until he had proof, that was an accusation to which he dare not give voice.

"Naaman, it isn't right that these others die," Daniel said slowly. "You must request an audience for me with Nebuchadnezzar. I will tell him that the God of Israel will reveal his dream to me, and its meaning."

"You are crazy. No man could do such a thing." Naaman retorted. This was too much! The fool had been told he had a death sentence hanging over his head, and yet believed he could do the impossible to save himself.

"Just do as I request, Naaman. My God will do the rest. Besides, look at it this way. If I am going to die, what difference does it make?" Daniel smiled at Naaman and then put his hand on Naaman's shoulder. In a serious voice, as if spoken between two close friends, and without the slightest hint of fear in his voice, Daniel concluded, "Do as I ask. All will be well."

CHAPTER 12

The Plot to Kill Daniel

REUBEN HAD NOT stopped to eat dinner since the courier had delivered the message from Troas.

Because he had taken care to code the message in Athbash, Reuben had had to spend the last several hours decoding the message. As he worked, Reuben thought again of the beauty of this simple, yet powerful cipher. No matter how many times he had to go through this process, he never lost his amazement for the ingeniousness with which the Hebrew scribes had used their language to disguise a code which could only be broken by those who held the key. To decode the message, Reuben worked with a device called an "Athbash disk," a wheel the size of a man's fist attached to a handle. An inner wheel held by spokes attached to the outer rim would rotate along an axis. On both the rims of the outer and inner wheels, the Hebrew

> **Athbash: The Hebrew Secret Code**
>
> There are at least three coded names in the book of Jeremiah. The code used appears to be a substitution cipher called Athbash (also spelled Atbash), as in A = T Ba = Sh — where the first letter is replaced with the last and the second is replaced with the second to last, etc. There are 22 letters in the Hebrew language. These letters can be arranged in such a way that secret codes can be sent. To decipher the codes, an Athbash Disk is used. Using two wheels, the letters on the outer circle can be matched with the letters on the inner circle.

alphabet appeared, with one difference. Along the outer wheel, the Hebrew alphabet read from right to left, with the first letter appearing at the top of the wheel. On the inner wheel, however, the letters read in reverse order, with the last letter at the top of the wheel, and read from left to right.

The key to deciphering the message was knowing exactly at what point to line up the inner and outer wheels, and then in which direction to rotate the inner wheel to begin the decoding process. Without that information - and the coding wheel - deciphering a message written in Athbash was nearly impossible. An added advantage to the use of the Athbash disk was that, to a non-Hebrew, the device could simply be explained as a "prayer wheel." Thus, if the Athbash disk were to be found with anyone other than a Hebrew, explaining how they got it would prove difficult. That was why Troas's elaborate plan called for passing his cousin off as a Hebrew.

Reuben had decoded almost all of the message; only a few words yet remained. The intent, however, was clear. So far, what Troas had said was: "Daniel must be assassinated. Jehoiakim has learned that Daniel will ask Nebuchadnezzar to install Zedekiah as king and depose Jehoiakim. Gain our friend's help. Tell them the assassination is an internal Hebrew affair."

Reuben worked quickly to decode the remaining phrase, smiling to himself at the beauty of Troas's plan. Quickly, he changed his clothing to something more suitable for an audience with Timnah.

"From your point of view, what you say makes sense," Timnah said slowly, choosing her words carefully. "Ever since Nebuchadnezzar has returned in defeat from Migdol, Daniel has opposed Haman at every turn at court. And now, he seeks to depose Jehoiakim and convince Nebuchadnezzar to install Zedekiah, his half-brother, as king. I can see why you believe Daniel has turned his back on his people and must be killed."

Reuben had gone straight to Timnah's home after he had finished decoding the message. Troas's motive for enlisting her support was quite clear. Because of her special relationship with Haman, he had no doubt that if Timnah could be convinced of the need to kill Daniel, she would in turn enlist the aid of Nebuchadnezzar's High Priest. While Reuben was right in that analysis, she had to make sure that killing Daniel would also benefit her people. "Before I can help you, I must be very certain of your answer to one question: Why should Ashkelon care who is king of Judah, and help you kill Daniel?"

"We both know that Haman is against having exiles from the conquered lands here in Babylon," Reuben began. "Even Naaman is said to be against it. Among the Hebrews, we believe that Babylon, not Egypt, is the greater evil - that Nebuchadnezzar is our nemesis, and Daniel is his agent. If Daniel is allowed to consolidate his power base at court under the guise of quieting the civil unrest in this realm, who will be able to stop him? Beware his true motives, Timnah. Daniel secretly plots the destruction of your people!"

Timnah had to admit to herself, that analysis rang true. Were she in Daniel's place, she would do <u>exactly</u> the same thing. She fought to suppress her emotions, her hatred for *those* people. Timnah needed Reuben, and therefore needed him to believe her motives for helping the Hebrews eliminate the traitor from their midst was borne of pure motives. She thought again of the Greek, Troas, and his message for her father. "I will help you, and let me tell you why. Just before Nebuchadnezzar attacked our city, a man named Troas came to tell us of an alliance that was being formed to fight with Egypt against Babylon. Were you aware of this?"

"No, this is the first I've heard of such an idea," Reuben lied.

"I didn't want to listen at the time, but now I see that he was right. I will go to Haman tomorrow evening and see what I might learn.

It may be that we can enlist his help against Daniel, for I know that he hates him. Thank you for coming. Go now."

Reuben rose to leave, and Shala escorted him to the door. He turned, and handing her a pouch of silver coins, said, "I will contact you soon. You have done well," and left. As soon as he was gone, Timnah called Shala to her. Before heeding her mistresses' call, Shala hid the pouch in a pocket of her robe.

"It is time that we began to put our plan to work," she told Shala. "Long ago, when we were brought to this place, I asked you to select cell leaders and charge them to keep watch for when we might plan our escape. You have done so?"

"Yes, my Queen."

"Good. Shala, I want you to send the word to be on the watch. Go and report back to me once we have our people in place." Timnah watched as Shala left to do her bidding. This was a delicate situation into which she had inserted herself. She said a silent prayer to Dagon to give her victory in revenge of her father's death, and her people's enslavement.

"Grandpa, a little while ago, Daniel told Naaman to get him an 'audience' with King Nebuchadnezzar. What does 'audience' mean?" Josiah sat patiently, looking up at his grandfather, waiting expectantly for an answer.

"That's an excellent question, Josiah! Think of when you have a Christmas program at your school, and all the children sing. Who all comes to listen to you and your classmates sing?" Grandpa beamed at grandson number three, eager to help him understand.

"Well, you and Nai Nai were there. And so were Mom and Dad. That was a lot of fun, Grandpa!"

"That's right. All those people who came to watch you, they are what we call an 'audience.' Their job is to listen to you. Your job is to sing to them."

Josiah thought for a moment, and then asked: "Is Daniel going to sing to King Nebuchadnezzar?"

"Ha, ha!" Grandpa belly laughed. "No. But when Daniel asks for an audience with king Nebuchadnezzar, what he means is that he would like to come and speak to the king. He will be an audience of one person."

"Grandpa, would anything happen to Daniel if King Nebuchadnezzar got mad at what Daniel had to say?" Nadia had decided to follow up on Josiah's question.

Grandpa looked at her for a long moment, thinking about how to answer her. Finally, he said: "Yes, Nadia, it is very possible that King Nebuchadnezzar would have done something terrible to Daniel. In those days, it was illegal to even speak to the king unless he spoke first to you first. Do you remember the story of Esther, when her uncle Mordecai wanted her to go and speak to the king?"

"Yes! I remember," answered Isaiah excitedly. "She was afraid that if she just went and told the king the message Mordecai wanted her to deliver, she could be killed. It was forbidden to speak to the king unless the king first asked you to speak."

"Let me tell you, if Grandpa tried that around here and I had to ask his permission to talk, he'd be the one in a heap of trouble." Nai Nai had opened the door to check on Grandpa and the kids. She winked at Grandpa before turning back to the them. "How about a break for some hot chocolate before Grandpa continues with the story? I'm making some for Hope and I thought I'd ask the rest of you if you wanted some."

"Yay!" all three of the children screamed and scrambled out of their chairs to go into the kitchen with their grandmother.

CHAPTER 13

Nebuchadnezzar Summons Daniel

T HAT SURE WAS good hot chocolate, Nai Nai," said Isaiah as he, Nadia and Josiah came back into the Sunroom.

"Thank you, Isaiah. You kids have a good time listening to Grandpa's story. I'm going to take Hope down the hall and put her to bed. It's time for her to go to sleep."

"But I can stay up with Isaiah and Nadia, right Nai Nai?" asked Josiah.

"Yes, for now. We'll see how long you last," she replied.

Just then Grandpa entered the room, dressed again in his costume, ready to continue his story. "Ok! It's time for you all to learn about Nebuchadnezzar's dream," he announced and took his place to continue the story. As Nai Nai closed the door behind her, Grandpa opened The Chronicles of Belteshazzar, and began to read:

In the fourth year of King Nebuchadnezzar, the Powers of Light battled the forces of darkness in the Heavenly realms. To Daniel, the God of Heaven revealed the secret things. Thus, in that year, a prophecy of future things to come was given to King Nebuchadnezzar II of Babylon in a dream. To Daniel of Jerusalem was given the task of revealing its meaning.

The Chronicles of Belteshazzar

Arriving at the palace, Daniel waited outside the great meeting hall. Naaman had gone ahead to request that Nebuchadnezzar meet with Daniel. It was forbidden for anyone to directly seek an audience with the king. Under Babylonian law, the king must first summon the individual into his presence. Daniel was content to let Naaman intercede for him. Finally, the door to the meeting hall opened, and Daniel was escorted inside. Haman, along with other members of Nebuchadnezzar's court, awaited him. Daniel walked beside Naaman and approached Nebuchadnezzar.

"Naaman has brought your petition to us, and so I have granted you an audience. Will you declare the content of my dream and its meaning to me?" Nebuchadnezzar stood, fists balled and pressed into either hip. Behind him, Haman glared at Daniel so intently, it seemed lightning bolts would leap from his eyes.

"Oh King, live forever!" Daniel said, bowing to his knee. "The interpretation of dreams is not in me, or any man. However, my God will reveal to me what Nebuchadnezzar has dreamed and its meaning. Give your servant one day, and I will provide you the answers you seek."

Nebuchadnezzar nodded to Daniel and took his seat. "Go then, and return here tomorrow morning at this same time to declare my dream, and I will richly reward you. Fail, and you will die."

Daniel rose and took his leave of Nebuchadnezzar to find his friends and pray. Naaman watched him as he left. Only hours ago, he had been sent to kill him. Now, Naaman would have to make doubly sure that Daniel would live another twenty four hours.

"We must act more quickly than we had planned," Haman spat the words from his mouth as he paced the floor.

"Tomorrow morning, Daniel will declare Nebuchadnezzar's dream. He must be killed tonight!"

Haman's servant, Reuben, sat as calmly as he could, given the circumstances. Whether or not he believed Daniel could declare and interpret the king's dream, Haman did, and that was that. "I have selected my men with care."

Haman smiled and went to a small chest in a corner of the room. From it, he withdrew four pieces of parchment, each rolled into a small scroll. All had been sealed with hot wax, with the insignia of the House of Ashkelon stamped into the wax. Each letter conveyed a forged command to its recipient to kill Daniel. The assassination was to take place at three in the morning, when the soldiers guarding Daniel would change. Haman would arrange to have the guards desert their posts, giving the assassins the opening they needed to kill Daniel. He gave the letters to his servant. "How did you select the assassins?"

Reuben reached out and took the letters. "It was most easy. I have a spy in the Queen of Ashkelon's apartment. Her name is Shala; she is the queen's servant. She supplied me with their top people. Once Daniel is dead, we will be able to accuse the Ashkelonites in his murder. It will lead to mass rioting. In the turmoil, you will be able to seize control from Nebuchadnezzar."

Haman smiled. "This stupid dream of Nebuchadnezzar's has forced me to speed up my timetable, but yes, you are quite right. Now go - there is little time to prepare for what must be done tonight."

Reuben bowed and left. Haman watched him go, then turned to look out his window. He spread his hands and leaned on the window sill and gazed out to the southeast. "Even now, Elam, I call on you to come to my aide. In a week, Babylon will have a new king!"

Clouds raced by underneath him. Flying effortlessly through the sky, Daniel descended to earth. Below him, it appeared that the surface of the earth moved with blinding speed - no, not the earth itself, but what was upon it. Cities rose and fell. The land changed in patches from forest, to grassland, to desert. Clouds of smoke would cover the cities, and then disappear as quickly as they had come. As he flew, Daniel saw a great statue, like none he had ever seen before. It was made of various elements – gold, silver, bronze, iron, and clay. It was as though ...

Daniel awoke, and knew that the Lord had given him the dream.

Throughout the day, Daniel had secluded himself to pray and to read the scrolls his father had given him. He had asked his friends to pray for him as well. As he had meditated, the day wore on into evening. Sometime during the night, Daniel had fallen asleep. Grasping his lamp, he quickly lit it and looked down at the scroll of Moses he'd been reading before nodding off. There before him lay the passage over which he'd been meditating.

Look, today I have set before you life and death, depending on whether you obey or disobey. I have commanded you today to love the Lord your God and to follow his paths and to keep his laws, so that you will live and become a great nation, and so that the Lord your God will bless you and the land you are about to possess.

Fully awake, Daniel dressed himself and went to his window. Judging by the night sky, it was around three in the morning. He had remained in his room all day long and felt the need to get out and walk around. The Lord had revealed to Daniel Nebuchadnezzar's dream, and he wanted to go for a walk to think through its meaning and to give thanks.

Exiting his chambers, Daniel made his way down a hallway which would lead him to one of the palace's inner courtyards. Daniel's thoughts focused solely on the dream, but even had he not been preoccupied with the vision he had just seen, Daniel was not the type to notice that the guard who should have been posted outside his door was missing. As he rounded a corner, Daniel stopped to take a ladle hanging from a large jug of water. Dipping the ladle into the jug, he took a long drink of the cool, wet liquid. Refreshed, he wiped a few stray droplets from his lips. Daniel was about to replace the ladle when he heard a low whisper, followed by footsteps, coming from the direction of his chambers. At first, Daniel thought it was the guard who had been stationed outside his door - and then froze, suddenly realizing that *there had been no guard* when he had left his chambers.

Quickly, in the dimness of the shadows, Daniel scanned the courtyard grounds. Built in the shape of a square, each side was approximately thirty yards long. An inner walkway underneath a balcony traversed the full length of the courtyard's perimeter, with cylindrical pillars spaced out about every six yards. Daniel had entered at the northeast corner of the courtyard and the only other exit lay diagonal across the courtyard at the southwest end. Daniel was about to make a run for it across the lawn to the other end, but then realized he would be an easy target for anyone stationed on the roof of the perimeter.

He turned and began to make his way along the inner perimeter. Behind him, he heard the clank of swords being pulled from their scabbards, and the heavy breathing of the men who held them. From behind a pillar, Daniel turned to look back, and saw four men begin to fan out across the courtyard, two coming in his direction, the other two moving to cover the northwest quadrant of the courtyard. He would have to make a run for it.

Daniel bolted from behind the pillar where he had been hiding towards the other exit at the southwest corner of the courtyard. He could hear footsteps approaching rapidly from the rear, gaining on him. He got to the exit of the courtyard, and came to an abrupt halt just in time to avoid colliding with the three men who emerged from the shadows of the gateway.

CHAPTER 14

Naaman to the Rescue

THIS NIGHT HAD been a strange one, and Naaman had not been able to sleep. A fog hung in the air as he decided to make his way to the guard house where the Captain of the Night Watch kept a log of palace guard assignments. Looking through the log, he came to Daniel's name, and saw that the posting assignment had been marked through. When Naaman had inquired as to the meaning of this, the Captain of the Night Watch said he had received orders not to post a guard for the watch.

That had triggered the mad rush that Naaman and the two soldiers who had been available were now on their way to Daniel's quarters. Only Naaman had the authority to approve a change in the Night Watchman's posting assignment. As they emerged through the gate into the courtyard, a figure narrowly missed colliding with them. Naaman looked closely at the man, suddenly realizing that the fugitive before them was Daniel.

Naaman didn't need to ask Daniel any questions - the reason for Daniel's sudden appearance was almost upon them. As one man moving in a fluid motion, Naaman and the other two soldiers drew their swords to meet the onrushing attackers, while Daniel flattened himself against a wall. The three formed a triangle, the base of which was the wall behind them where Daniel stood, slowly comprehending what was happening about him.

Naaman met the attacker directly in front of him. His opponent brought his sword down at Naaman's head with a mighty two-handed blow. Naaman parried, lifting his sword nearly parallel to the ground to deflect the blow. Once the two blades had met, Naaman stepped to his right and brought his sword in an arc from right to left, slicing through the man's midsection. In shock, Naaman's enemy stood for a second, watching his life's blood flow out of him before collapsing on the cobble stones.

But Naaman did not have time to watch the man die. Two attackers were pressing in on one of Naaman's men. He raced to his comrade's aide, driving his sword into the back of one of the attackers while the Babylonian soldier, though wounded himself, felled the other assassin.

From behind them, Daniel cried out, locked in a fight for his life with the remaining assassin who had already killed Naaman's other guard. Daniel had managed to grab both of the man's wrists, but now the attacker had freed his sword hand and raised his weapon with the intent of delivering a mortal blow to Daniel's skull.

But instead of feeling the steel of the assassin's blade, he was showered with the man's blood as the attacker's wrist, now a bloody stump, swung past Daniel. The attacker's sword, still held in the clutches of his right hand, fell to the ground, severed from its owner's arm by Naaman's expert blow. Naaman grabbed the man, writhing in agony. "We will keep this one alive to tell us who ordered this attempt on your life. Are you all right, Daniel?"

"Yes, I think so," Daniel said. "Thank you." Daniel set to binding the man's wrist to prevent him from bleeding to death, while Naaman inspected him for other weapons. Then he attended to the wounds of his other soldier. Just then, four more of Naaman's palace guards arrived.

Naaman barked orders to the arriving guards. "Take this man and lock him in the deepest dungeon we have. Tell no one that he is alive. Take the bodies of these others and search them for any clues as to their identity, then burn them. If anyone asks, tell them there were four bodies that were disposed of. When the time is right, this dog will reveal who masterminded the plot to kill Daniel."

Naaman turned to Daniel. "You shall spend the rest of the night in my quarters, and we shall triple the guard around you. Someone does not want you to interpret Nebuchadnezzar's dream tomorrow."

Daniel didn't speak, but quietly followed Naaman to his quarters.

Early in the morning, in the predawn light, Naaman roused his house guest. The two ate their breakfast in silence, and then made their way to the palace of the King. As Naaman entered the Court of Nebuchadnezzar with Daniel at his side, he felt the eyes of Haman pierce the two of them. More than ever, Naaman believed that the Chief Priest had something to do with the attempt on Daniel's life the night before. But that was a matter that would have to await further investigation.

"Daniel, the appointed hour has arrived," said Nebuchadnezzar. "Are you able to tell me my dream and interpret its meaning?"

All eyes focused on Daniel. Naaman didn't know why, but he knew that Daniel would be able to answer the king's question.

"None of your magi, astrologers, or wizards can tell you such things, but there is a God in heaven who does," Daniel responded. "He has told you in your dream what will happen in the future. In your dream, you saw a huge statue of a man, shining brilliantly, frightening and terrible. It was awesome to behold. The head was made of purest gold, its chest and arms were made of silver, its belly and thighs of brass, its legs of iron. Part of the feet were also made of iron, and part of clay. But as you watched, a rock cut from the mountainside came hurtling toward the statue and crushed the feet of iron and clay, smashing them to bits. The whole statue collapsed, its pieces crushed as small as chaff. But as the wind blew the pieces of the statue all away, the rock that knocked the statue down became a great mountain that covered the whole earth."

While everyone else in the room had their eyes glued to Daniel, Naaman watched Haman's reaction. Everyone in the Court was aware that Daniel had survived an assassination attempt on his life. But only Naaman knew the full story, and he was staying silent to see if Haman would react upon seeing Daniel alive. The Chief Priest appeared as though he would speak, but before he could do so, Nebuchadnezzar was on his feet. Quickly, he descended the steps to where Daniel stood and said, "This is indeed the dream I had. Tell me, what does it mean?"

"Your Majesty, the meaning of your dream is this," Daniel said, drawing a deep breath before proceeding. "You are a king over many kings, for the God of heaven has given you your kingdom, power strength and glory. You rule the farthest provinces, and even the animals are under your control, as God decreed. You are that head of gold."

"But after your kingdom has come to an end, another world power will arise to take your place. This empire will be inferior to yours. Following that kingdom, yet a third great power - represented by the bronze belly of the statue - will rise to rule the world. Again, this kingdom too shall be replaced by a fourth kingdom made of iron. The meaning of the feet and toes, part iron, part clay, show that later on, this fourth kingdom will be divided. Part of it will be as strong as iron, some as weak as clay. While these kingdoms will try to strengthen themselves by forming alliances through intermarriage, this will not succeed, for iron and clay do not adhere to one another."

"What of the great rock of which you spoke? What can it possibly be?" interrupted Haman, barely able to contain himself as Daniel interpreted the dream.

"During the reign of the kings represented by the feet and toes, the God of Heaven will establish a kingdom that will never be destroyed. It will shatter all these kingdoms into nothingness, but it shall stand forever. This is the meaning of the rock cut from the mountain without human hands that will crush the great statue. The God of Heaven has shown Nebuchadnezzar what will happen. Its fulfillment is as certain as my description of it." Daniel concluded his presentation and stood silent before Nebuchadnezzar.

Nebuchadnezzar turned and slowly ascended the stairs to his throne. All stood in silence, awaiting what Nebuchadnezzar would say. Finally, he looked at Daniel and said, "You have been one of the Magi, but now you have shown yourself to be the greatest of the Magi. From this day forth, you will be the Chief Scribe. And your name shall be changed to Belteshazzar, the "Diviner of the Way of the Gods."

"But your Highness, he is a foreigner. You cannot do this!" Haman interrupted. Immediately, he realized that he had spoken out of turn, but it was too late to retract his words.

Nebuchadnezzar whirled to face Haman. "Does the Chief Priest challenge the right of the king to select his Chief Scribe? You have control of the temple, High Priest. I am sure that you will do all that is necessary to ensure that I continue to bring glory to Marduk, and that the temple coffers are full."

Turning to Daniel, Nebuchadnezzar said, "From this day forth, to commemorate my dream, you shall be in charge of rebuilding the Temple of Etemenanki. In that temple, you shall build a room dedicated to your God. While the temple shall be a place of worship to Marduk, there within that special chamber shall the God of Belteshazzar be worshipped."

The ziggurat of Etemenanki stretched 300 feet into the air beside the temple of Esagila. Nearly ninety years ago, the Assyrian king Sennacherib had destroyed the temple. Only recently, Nebuchadnezzar had completed the rebuilding of the temple to Haman's specifications. The Hebrews who had been brought to the land of the Chaldeans spread the rumor amongst themselves that it was indeed the fabled Tower of Babel written of by Moses in the sacred scrolls.

Even Naaman was surprised by this command. The temple of Etemenanki was devoted to Marduk, along with his consort, Sarpanitum. The main shrine of Marduk at the temple was a chamber whose interior was completely overlain with gold. Within the shrine was a large golden image of Marduk and Sarpanitum, while other images flanked the divine couple, tending to their needs. Would this room to be devoted to Daniel's God be equally magnificent? And what would Haman do regarding this clear infringement on his responsibilities?

As Naaman mulled over these thoughts, a guard came and whispered into his ear. Listening to his guard, he looked up at Haman, for the news that the guard was bringing him spoke of a disaster only a select few could have triggered. Fighting had broken out between the Hebrews and the Ashkelonites within the city walls. On the same day - the same day - raiders from Elam had attacked Susa, less than a week's march to the southeast.

And then he thought of something. The only place where rioting was NOT happening was in the two neighborhoods where he had tested Daniel's idea for a Council of Exiles to meet and discuss their issues. Naaman approached the king and, kneeling at his feet, waited for Nebuchadnezzar to command him to speak.

"Rise, Naaman, what is on your heart," asked Nebuchadnezzar.

"My king, fighting has broken out in the city between Hebrew and Ashkelonite. Somehow, news that Daniel is dead has gotten out and caused the Hebrews to seek revenge. If My Lord pleases, then once we have quieted the city, I seek your permission to create a Council of Exiles living among us. I have worked with Daniel to test this idea as a way to help keep the peace. It has worked in the two neighborhoods where we have tried it during this uprising. Nothing has happened in those sectors."

"Granted," replied Nebuchadnezzar. About to turn away, he noticed that Naaman had not risen as he had expected. "There is more?"

"Yes, My Lord. Raiders *from* Elam have attacked Susa this very day.

It is as if they knew we would be distracted here in Babylon, and have deliberately invaded our Southern Capital. What is your command!" Naaman looked up, waiting for his king's response.

Nebuchadnezzar eyed the people of his court, his eyes resting on Daniel. After a moment's thought, he turned to Shamgar and said, "General Shamgar, learn more about the situation in Susa, and then take up to half your army to beat back the forces of Elam." As Shamgar bowed and left to carry out his orders, Nebuchadnezzar next turned to Naaman. "You lead a squadron of guards to restore order. Once that is accomplished, find out who is behind this - I shall have their head."

Naaman bowed, but before turning to leave, he looked at Haman and, acting on a hunch said, "My men will find those who ordered this. Whomever is responsible likely does not realize that we still have one of the assassins. I swear, those behind this will pay!" As Naaman walked out of the chambers he heard Haman almost succeed in stifling a curse.

After both Shamgar and Naaman had left, Nebuchadnezzar motioned to Daniel to come and join him. Together, they ascended the steps to walk out to the king's balcony. Putting his hand on Daniel's shoulder, Nebuchadnezzar leaned toward his new Chief Scribe and said, "Someone wants you dead. When Naaman has caught up with them, we will know why. Now, we must go and speak to the people so that they will know that you are still alive, and to proclaim the empire which you have foreseen."

CHAPTER 15

Ezekiel Visits Babylon

EZEKIEL HAD HEARD tales of Babylon, but actually seeing the city put all stories of its splendor to shame. Alternating figures of bulls and dragons greeted the caravan to which he'd attached himself as they entered the Gate of Ishtar. On the walls lining the interior of the city, frescoes of lions twenty feet long conveyed the power that was Babylon's. So this was the force God had unleashed to deliver His vengeance! Ezekiel was both terrified at the thought, but thrilled by the knowledge that he was somehow involved in the unfolding chain of events.

Because they had no idea what kind of eyes and ears Jehoiakim might have in this city, Jeremiah had instructed him to first seek out Abednego, Meshach and Shadrach. Most likely, they would be found in the Hebrew quarter of the city. For several hours, he wandered through the city, more out of a desire to explore than because he was lost. Once he came to the Hebrew quarter, he was struck by how clean and seemingly prosperous the new home of his countrymen was. Indeed, it appeared that they fared even better than those shopkeepers who plied their trade in Jerusalem!

After several inquiries, Ezekiel learned that his three friends shared an apartment above the shop of a flask merchant, for whom they worked. Close to the edge of the Hebrew quarter, it was near the western side of the Bridge of Heaven. After getting directions from a fish merchant, along with his supper, he proceeded to his destination.

It would be dark in a few hours, and Ezekiel looked forward to finding his friends soon. Finally, he came to the intersection where he had been told he would find the flask merchant's shop and his friends' apartment. As he was preparing to walk across the street, shouting erupted a block away. Ezekiel stopped and stared, as a fight broke out between a dozen or so youths, some carrying sticks. Giving into his curiosity, Ezekiel began to walk in the direction of the melee.

The fight was drawing a crowd, and Ezekiel soon found himself caught up in a riot. Clearly, some of the rioters were Hebrews, but there were individuals from other groups whom he did not recognize. He heard the clamor of horses to his left, and turned to see a troop of Babylonian guards ride up and begin to disburse the combatants. Those who resisted were arrested. Ezekiel realized this was the wrong place to be. Deciding to hurry back to his friends' home, he turned to leave - and was trapped in a net being dragged by two Babylonian horsemen. As Ezekiel was pulled along in the dragnet, several others joined him as they too were caught in its path.

"Release me! I have done nothing!" Ezekiel shouted through the shock and pain of being dragged over the cobble stone street.

"Quiet, pig, or I'll cut out your tongue!" a soldier cursed at him, taking a swing at Ezekiel with the flat of his sword, missing his head by a fraction of an inch. Ezekiel and his fellow prisoners ceased struggling. It became apparent that those rioters who had not been captured had quickly fled. The soldiers paid the escapees no interest, concentrating only on those they had rounded up. Faintly, but distinctly, Ezekiel heard a familiar voice as he lay tangled in the dragnet.

"Commander, release that one into my custody. I will vouch for him personally," said the voice of a young Hebrew man. Ezekiel fought against the bindings of the net, craning his neck to get a glimpse of the man. It was Shadrach!

"By whose authority should I do this?" snarled the corporal to whom the request had been made.

"By the authority of Belteshazzar, Chief Mage in the Court of Nebuchadnezzar," said Shadrach, displaying the broach of his cloak with Daniel's insignia - an eagle holding a seven-pronged candlestick. The soldier grumbled, but complied with Shadrach's request.

"Come, Ezekiel," said Shadrach softly as they finished untangling him. "Let's get you to safety among friends. We have much to discuss." Ezekiel allowed himself to be led away from the scene of the riot to the safety of his friends' home.

"As you have seen, unrest among the exile groups is growing. Daniel has argued for a forum where leaders of the different groups can meet and discuss their differences, but Haman, Nebuchadnezzar's High Priest, has forbidden it," Abednego said as he placed a plate of food in front of Ezekiel. "We await news of the outcome of the attack against Egypt. There is no telling what will happen if the people find that Nebuchadnezzar was defeated. Have you any news, Ezekiel?"

Ezekiel chewed and swallowed his bite of food. "There had been no news of the battle when I left, though we knew that Babylon was moving against Egypt." He paused to look at his friends before proceeding. He was surprised that they asked of the fate of Nebuchadnezzar instead of their homeland, even of their families. "Have you had any word of what is happening back home?"

"We have been most unkind," said Meshack. "There must be something of great importance back home, otherwise you would not be here, Ezekiel. Tell us about our families and friends. How is Jeremiah?" The three listened as Ezekiel told them of their loved ones, and the growing apostasy of the people under the reign of Jehoiakim. As the friends spoke, a knock came at the door. Shadrach got up and went to the door. He opened it, and Daniel walked in and embraced his old friend.

"I came as soon as I heard you were here! God has truly blessed you," said Daniel as he held Ezekiel's shoulders in his hands. Ezekiel gave an abbreviated version of what he had just told the other three. Finally, Daniel looked across at his friend and said: "I know that you are here for an important reason. Please, tell us what has brought you to Babylon."

"When we learned you had been made a Mage in the court of Nebuchadnezzar, Jeremiah knew that it must mean the Lord was giving Judah a way to redeem itself. The Lord has shown Jeremiah the death of Jehoiakim, and he has sent me to tell you," Ezekiel said. "At the appropriate time, Jeremiah wants you to speak with Nebuchadnezzar and have him place Zedekiah on the throne after him."

Daniel began to open his mouth to speak, and then thought better of what he wanted to say. Zedekiah was fifteen years younger than his half brother, Jehoiakim. Daniel knew that Jeremiah had a fondness for Zedekiah. For years in the Court of Zedekiah's father, Josiah, Jeremiah had tutored the young prince. Daniel suspected that it was because of that relationship that Jeremiah placed his faith in the young prince. But there also existed a practical political reason for Jeremiah's request. Ever since Josiah had died in his attack on Pharaoh Necho at Megiddo years ago, many had speculated that Jehoiakim had conspired with Egypt to orchestrate his father's death. Therefore, so long as Jehoiakim held the throne of David, he would owe allegiance to his benefactor, Egypt. The same would be true of Jehoiakim's son, Jehoiachin.

Daniel realized that Zedekiah didn't have a similar history of allegiance to Egypt. Combined with the prince's tendency to listen to the last advisor to speak with him, it was Daniel's opinion that if Nebechadnezzar made Zedekiah king of Judah instead of Jehoiachin, Zedekiah would prove to be an unfaithful ally of Babylon. It was for that reason that Daniel didn't believe Zedekiah would prove to be any better a king than Jehoiakim. Having spent nearly two years in the Court of Nebuchadnezzar, Daniel had come to realize that the agenda of the Lord seldom made it onto the political agenda of mere men. Daniel decided that he did not wish to reveal this difference of perspective from his mentor - at least, not yet.

"When the time comes, I will do as you ask," Daniel finally answered. "Ezekiel, as much as I am overjoyed to see you, I ask that you return home at the earliest opportunity. The strife between the exile communities grows, as you witnessed for yourself today. When Nebuchadnezzar returns, I must confront him over the policies of his chief counselor, Haman. If this strife is not checked, it will tear Babylon apart."

Ezekiel nodded in assent. Daniel smiled, marveling silently at the difference in their relationship since he had left Jerusalem and come to Babylon. When they had parted, of the two, Ezekiel had been the leader. Somewhere along the way, he had grown up. In that instant, Daniel realized that reality for what it was. He didn't want the responsibility for his people that he knew God was shifting to his shoulders. The last few hours had already loaded his plate with more than he felt he could bear.

"I will go now. Pressing matters await me at Court. Heed my words, Ezekiel, and give everyone back in Jerusalem my love."

"I will, my friend," Ezekiel said as he hugged Daniel good-bye.

Daniel excused himself and left. In the night sky, he saw a full moon overhead. Joining his escort, he climbed into the carriage and prepared for the ride back to the palace. In two days, Nebuchadnezzar would return with his defeated army. Riders had arrived only hours ago to advise Daniel of Babylon's defeat at Migdol. He bowed his head in prayer to ask the Lord for guidance in how to serve both his people and the King of Babylon. While the Hebrews would like nothing better than to see the Babylonian Empire collapse, it was Daniel's duty to help try to preserve it. Not for the first time, Daniel asked his God why he had been placed in this impossible situation.

Isaiah had listened closely to the story, but there was something that had been bugging him. Finally, he realized what it was. "Grandpa, was there really a Chief Priest named Haman?"

"Isaiah, that's a great question! There probably wasn't a Haman exactly. But, here's what we do know. We know that during different parts of its history, Babylon had a King who ruled over all the non-religious parts of the kingdom, and a chief priest who was responsible for all the things related to the Babylonian religion, its temples, and sacrifices. Also, there were times in Babylon's history where the same person was both the King and the Chief Priest. But there were also times when these two jobs were done by different people. And when that happened, there could be political fights about who oversaw what. Now, during the time Nebuchadnezzar was King, there were two different people doing the job of Chief Priest and King.

"What do you mean about 'political fights,' Grandpa?" Nadia had decided to jump into the conversation. "What's the difference between a political fight and a sword fight?"

"Ha, Ha! Sometimes, not much, Nadia!" Grandpa had a good chuckle at the girl's question. "Throughout human history, people who oversee things have power over others, and sometimes they try to get even more power for their own greedy uses. That means taking power from others."

Grandpa thought for a moment on how he might explain this better to his grandchildren, and then hit on an idea.

"Do you remember watching the 3 Musketeers last week?"

"Yah, that was cool," piped up Josiah. "They did lots of sword fighting."

"Yes, that's right," answered Grandpa. "But do you remember who the Three Musketeers worked for?"

"King Louis XIII," promptly replied Isaiah.

Grandpa smiled and pressed on with his analogy. "That's right! But do you also remember who they were fighting against?"

"Cardinal Rich!" replied Josiah.

"You mean Cardinal Rich*elieu*," chimed in Nadia, careful to emphasize the last part of the Cardinal's name.

As if a lightbulb had just gone off in his head, Isaiah supplied the answer to his own question. "Hey! A Cardinal is a Priest, and an important one at that! Richelieu was a chief priest just like Haman."

Grandpa beamed at his three grandchildren. Thankful they had recently watched the Three Musketeers, and that the analogy was still fresh in their minds. Finally, he said; "Yes, Cardinal Richelieu was actually an evil, greedy man, just like my imaginary Chief Priest Haman. But, there's one other thing.

"What?" asked Nadia.

"Scholars – those are people who have studied this sort of thing a lot – say that King Nebuchadnezzar had to put down a revolt in his kingdom sometime between 595 and 592 B.C. It was a very serious problem he faced."

"How serious?" asked Isaiah.

"Well, to find out, I need to continue with the story."

CHAPTER **16**

The Feast of Akitu

A s GRANDPA WAS preparing to resume the story, Nai Nai came into the room. "Hope is asleep, so I thought I would come and join you all for the story."

"Great to have you, Nai Nai! You can make sure I tell the story right! Now, where was I? Oh, here we are!" Grandpa opened The Chronicles of Belteshazzar to where had he had left off, and started to read.

> *In the first year of the reign of King Zedekiah, the second wave of exiles was taken into Babylon. In a scheme intended to remove the Lord's Anointed from the Court of Nebuchadnezzar, Haman the Chief Priest ordered that even the exiles must bow down to the gods of the Babylonians. Of all the Hebrews exiled in Babylon, only three refused to obey. Through the faithfulness of a few, the gods of the Babylonians were shamed, and the arrogance of Haman shaken.*
>
> The Chronicles of Belteshazzar

She had to find Daniel. The consequences of her not finding him would mean Haman would indeed triumph.

Already, Nebuchadnezzar had entered the city gates with his second wave of exiles. Timnah, Queen of the Philistines, smiled to herself, seeing full well the irony in her attempting to save the life of this Hebrew. In speaking to several who knew his habits, Timnah had chosen the one spot where Daniel might go to be able to pray and watch the entire city at the same time. Fortunately, she was in good enough physical shape to make the journey without too much loss of time. As she reached the sixth stage of the ziggurat Etemenanki, she hoped Dagon would find favor in her. If Daniel were not to be found in his prayer chamber, she did not know where she would look next.

At five feet ten inches, she carried her lithe, athletic frame erect, not stooped like some overly tall girls trying to mask their height. Her long, black flowing hair framed her somewhat slanted eyes which flashed a glint of cunning intelligence. Her every move communicated strength and aloofness. She came to the door of the shrine to Daniel's God. Pausing to look at the gold relief design, Timnah studied the picture contained therein - a ram with its horns locked in the branches of a thorn bush. She made a mental note to ask Daniel what it meant when the time was right. As quickly as the urge to wonder about the design had come, it left. Timnah turned to the job at hand and, pulling the handle, opened the door. To her relief, she found Daniel, on his knees, praying.

"Daniel," she said softly, not wanting to interrupt him. While the two had met on social occasions, they had rarely spoken to one another. Though the circumstances and their lack of familiarity made what Timnah had to do doubly difficult, she could not retreat now from the urgency to act. "You are in great danger. Please, you must come with me and do as I say."

Daniel turned and looked up at the woman, recognizing her face, though searching his memory momentarily to recall her name. "You are Timnah, yes? What in the world ..."

"Yes, I am Timnah," she said cutting him off. "I have come to get you - you must leave with me now."

Daniel shook his head. "No, that's not possible. I'm sure whatever it is, it can wait," he replied.

"We do not have time to debate. Your life is in danger. You can remain here and die, or you can come with me and live. Which will it be?" Timnah stood in the doorway, hands balled into fists buried into her hips.

Daniel, realizing the woman meant business, rose and rolled up his prayer mat, sticking it in a corner of the shrine. Pushing the door shut behind them and locking it, Daniel began to follow her down the levels of the ziggurat. As they spiraled down the levels of the structure, Daniel finally broke the silence. "It must be something of grave importance to cause the Queen of Ashkelon to come and rescue me from an as yet unexplained threat. Before I go any further with you, you will have to tell me what danger it is I face."

Timnah, walking slightly ahead of him, stopped and turned to face Daniel. "In two days, the New Year festival celebration begins. Always before, all of the exile groups were required to remain in their quarters while the Chaldeans celebrated the rebirth of Marduk. However, Haman intends to request of Nebuchadnezzar that all the exiles be present at the time of the Poem of Creation ceremony. When all the Chaldeans bow down and worship their king as the risen Marduk, Haman will require all the exile peoples to bow down and worship too."

"But I could never do that!" Daniel said, shocked that after three years in Babylon, he and his fellow Hebrews might be required to partake of this annual ritual.

"And that is exactly what Haman expects," Timnah said tersely. "Your failure to bow down and worship Nebuchadnezzar will force the king to order your execution! It is why you must go to Nebuchadnezzar now, before Haman has a chance to make his wishes known to the king, to request leave to go up into the mountains. Tell him you want to go away to pray for him and for Babylon. Only if you are not here during the New Year's celebration will you be safe." Timnah grabbed his hand and began to walk at a near jog, dragging Daniel along.

Recovering from being pulled off balance, he quickly fell into step beside her, asking, "But what of the other Hebrews? What of my friends? What shall become of them?"

Timnah turned and looked into Daniel's eyes, an evil grin forming on the corners of her mouth. "You will just have to trust your god to protect them, won't you?" Even while she was helping this one Hebrew, she took sadistic pleasure in lashing him with her cutting words. Daniel lowered his gaze to the ground, concentrating on the task at hand.

As the two walked on in silence, Daniel's thoughts turned to the arrival of this new wave of Hebrew exiles. From atop Etemenanki, the train of Nebuchadnezzar's army and accompanying exiles could be seen to stretch into the distance. Concern for his own safety totally forgotten, Daniel looked forward to hearing the news from home. Daniel's yearning to see if any of his friends were among the arriving Hebrews grew with each passing step. But it would be at least a day, maybe two, before he would be able to speak with any newly arrived friends. Already, Nebuchadnezzar had entered the city at the head of the procession and was just entering the square of the palace when Timnah and Daniel arrived to greet him.

Haman stood at the top of the stairs leading to the palace awaiting Nebuchadnezzar. Timnah looked at him, and then grabbing Daniel by the arm, said, "You must act quickly. Go now and speak to Nebuchadnezzar before Haman has a chance to make his announcement."

Despite the push Timnah gave to propel him forward, Daniel walked up to Nebuchadnezzar's chariot in a casual and relaxed manner. Raising his hand in salute, Daniel said, "Hail great Nebuchadnezzar, ruler of the earth. Welcome home."

Nebuchadnezzar looked down at Daniel, the significance of what he had just done not being lost on anyone. It was the custom of the Chief Priest to be the first to formally greet the king when returning from a conquering expedition. "Thank you, Belteshazzar. It is good to be home in time for the New Year festivities. Do you have something you wish to say?"

Without hesitation, Daniel lifted up his arms and spoke. "Only that your humble servant asks permission to go into the mountains for ten days of fasting and prayer. There I shall ask the God of my people to bless Nebuchadnezzar, and to cause my people to honor and serve you."

Timnah glanced quickly in Haman's direction, saw him ball his fists at his side. Undecided as to what to say or do before Nebuchadnezzar responded, he lost his chance to intervene.

"By the gods, well spoken!" Nebuchadnezzar replied. Looking in Haman's direction, he continued, "Yes, go and offer prayers for me and my kingdom. Will this not be a fitting tribute to Marduk, Haman?"

Haman's face relaxed visibly when Nebuchadnezzar spoke to him. Timnah never ceased to be amazed how this man could change his expression and demeanor in the twinkling of an eye to fit the needs of the situation. Ever since her pledge to Naaman several months ago to watch Haman, she had asked herself repeatedly why she had failed to see the man for the chameleon he was? Truly, fools only see that which they wish to see - and she had been a fool.

"Great king, mighty Conqueror! Marduk will be honored. And as Daniel worships and prays in the mountains alone, let his people also bow down and worship Marduk as chief of the gods. Thus, let it be that on the sixth day of Akitu, the New Year's festival when you go to the New Year's temple, all of the people of Babylon - not just the Chaldeans - will bow down and worship Marduk. Let those who refuse to bow the knee to Marduk be thrown into a fiery furnace, their burned flesh offered up as a fragrant aroma to our god."

"Double glory be to me and the gods," shouted Nebuchadnezzar. Clearly impressed with the idea, Nebuchadnezzar led his train to the palace to bathe and refresh himself from his long march.

As Timnah watched Haman escort the king, Daniel returned to her, his face downcast. Glaring at him, she said, "Had you remained in the city during the Festival of Akitu, you too would have been made to bow the knee to Marduk. This you would never have done - and you would have died. Where is your gratitude? I have saved your life!"

Daniel looked at her, a deep sadness in his eyes. "Nearly all of my people will bow the knee to save their lives. Haman will have broken their resolve to worship Jehovah God alone. This is a terrible day."

"You conceited fool. Do you not think my people also cherish their religion just as do you? But we are realistic - our God will understand it was done under duress. You take yourself too seriously, Daniel."

> **Feast of Akitu**
>
> There are ancient tablets called the **Enuma Elish**, which tell the Babylonian **Poem of Creation**.
>
> This story was celebrated annually by carrying the gods down the **Processional Way**.
>
> This 12-day celebration was called the **Feast of Akitu**.
>
> During the Feast of Akitu, statues of the Babylonian Gods would have been brought down the **Euphrates River** and unloaded at the Processional Way.
>
> From there, they would have been carried into the city to the **Ziggurat of Esgalia**.

He smiled at her with the kind of sad, knowing smile a parent shows their little one when they have suffered harm. And then he said something that cut her to the quick. "You say that because you do not truly believe your god can save you. Our God can. Those who do not bow the knee and are cast into the fire will live. This is a time of testing for our people. We have always worshipped our God in a temple, but He wishes to build His temple in our hearts - my heart, and yours, Timnah. One day, Messiah will come, and in that day our God will write a new covenant on our hearts. His law will be within us, for He shall live in us. That covenant will be free for the asking for your people, for my people, for all people."

"Then why did you take my advice and go to Nebuchadnezzar, so that you will be gone when the rest of your people will be forced to bow done?," she shot back.

Daniel didn't attempt to hide the shame in his face. Finally, he answered her. "Because it was not until Haman spoke that I fully understood the test my God had designed. Let me explain by way of a story. Abraham was the founder of my people. Once, God demanded of him something which was unthinkable, yet Abraham obeyed without question. God commanded Abraham to take his son Isaac into the wilderness to be sacrificed. Abraham obeyed, even though he was afraid. But because he was faithful, God provided a ram to sacrifice in his son's place.

"The ram pictured on the door to the room I found you in?" Timnah asked, remembering the relief she had wondered about earlier.

"Yes, the very same. Too late, He revealed to me what must happen, and so I was not faithful as was the patriarch Abraham." Daniel lifted his hand to quiet the woman as she attempted to interrupt. "I thank you for your kindness, Timnah. You did what you did in order to save me, and that is what matters. I must go now to speak with some of my people, and then prepare to fulfill my vow."

Daniel took his leave, as Timnah stood staring at his backside. With a mixture of emotions running through her, she didn't know what to think. In any case, either this Daniel was a bumbling, self-deluded naive fool, or a mighty wizard. Of one thing she was certain: Never in her life had she met someone like him who was, well, genuinely kind and good.

The feast of Akitu was in its fifth day. Celebrated in the month the Hebrews called Nisan during the spring equinox, it marked Babylon's New Year celebration, exalting herself, her riches, her science, her king and her gods. For the last five days, the city had been engulfed in one unending carnival, interrupted with religious ceremonies conducted by the priests. All thought of the people's daily lives had been put aside as the priests focused their attention, between drunken parties, on what the New Year would hold if the city was blessed by Marduk.

At precisely sunrise of the sixth day, Haman walked out onto the second level of Esagila. Raising his arms, he began the Poem of Creation, crying out to Marduk:

Marduk, unequaled in thy wrath,
Marduk, kind King, Lord of the Lands,
Who makes the Great Gods favorable,
Lord of Kings, Light of Mankind,
Who dost allot portions,
Thou dost control oracles; with thine eyes thou dost give the law.
Lord of the lands of the city of Babylon,
Have mercy on the children of Babylon!

A ripple of cries went forth from the citizens of Babylon at the utterance of this portion of the poem. Then, with one voice, they cried out: "Call Marduk back to life!"

"It will not be long now," Meshach said to his two friends. "Look, here comes the barge carrying the statue of the god Anu, father of the Babylonian gods." Along with Shadrach and Abednego, Meshach watched as the great idol was brought to shore and off-loaded where Nebuchadnezzar sat at his gold table awaiting its arrival. The idol had been transported downstream from its shrine. This was the signal for every temple in Babylon to open. Out of each shrine all the gods of the city, both great and small, were brought out to join Nebuchadnezzar and Anu as they traveled down the Processional Way to Esgalia. The mass of priests, idols, officials, scribes and soldiers choked the Sacred Way as they transported the idols. Behind them, the masses of the people followed, all intoxicated with mystic faith. Behind them, soldiers herded members of the various exile communities forward. Because they had been made overseers under the authority of Daniel, Meshach, Shadrach and Abednego led the procession of the Hebrews toward the ziggurat of Etemenanki, and beyond it, Esgalia, the temple of Marduk.

With Nebuchadnezzar at the head of the procession, he stopped at the base of Etemenanki. There, priests brought a white bull to him. Dazed from a drug so that it would pose no danger to the king, it stood by the altar awaiting its end. Taking a long gold-hilted knife, Nebuchadnezzar cut its throat. In a stupor, the bull stood for a few moments as its life's blood spurted from its jugular before collapsing. "O divine bull, thou art the shining light which illuminates the darkness!" Nebuchadnezzar intoned.

The priests took the bull and burned it. As the flames leaped up to consume the bull's carcass, white smoke rose into the air. In unison, the people behind Nebuchadnezzar chanted, as the king cried out, "Come out, Bel-Marduk! The king awaits you!"

"This is the moment we have awaited," Abednego said. "When the time comes, we must do as Daniel told us and not bow down." The other two nodded their assent, and watched.

In response to Nebuchadnezzar, Haman recited the last part of the Creation Poem, taking now the voice of Marduk:

> *If I, your avenger*
> *Must make you live,*
> *Exalt and proclaim my destiny.*
> *Let the word of my mouth, even as yours, establish destinies.*

This was the signal to the musicians to strike their cymbals and chimes. Along the east wall of the ziggurat Etemenanki, thousands of servants in unison lifted placards into place. When seen from afar, they displayed the symbol of Babylon, a lion with eagle's wings. The face on the lion was that of Nebuchadnezzar, their king. The people bowed down to worship their god-king, who was now the god Marduk incarnate on earth, as Haman called out:

I will Proclaim his might,
Sing his strength,
Celebrate his valor!
Marduk the compassionate, the merciful,
To whom it is profitable to turn!
He it is who hearkens to my prayer,
Who grants the favors which appease the hearer!

Amidst the noise and shouting, Nebuchadnezzar turned with his new queen, the statue of Marduk behind them, to lead the march back across the Processional Way. Along both sides of the road, as the music played and the priests chanted, all the people bowed down to worship the image of Nebuchadnezzar upon the wall of Etemenanki.

All except the three Hebrews. As Nebuchadnezzar came upon them, he stopped and pointed at them. "You are servants in the Court of Babylon," he said. "I command you to bow down as have all the rest, or die."

Shadrach, the eldest of the three, stepped forward to speak for all of them. "Great Nebuchadnezzar, King of Babylon, what you ask is impossible for us to perform. Do with us as you will. Our God, whom we serve, is able to deliver us from the furnace you have prepared. But even if He chooses not to do so, Oh King, know that we can never bow down and serve any image of any god." When he had finished, Shadrach stepped back to stand with the others. They stood in silence, knowing that their actions invited Nebuchadnezzar to order their deaths.

Finally, Nebuchadnezzar could stand it no longer. "You will be thrown into the furnace which Haman has prepared," he said, his voice trembling with rage. "Tonight, at the rising of the Full Moon, your charred corpses shall illuminate the feasting that all Babylon shall partake in." As a dozen guards knocked the three to the ground to bind and carry them off, Nebuchadnezzar led the Procession of the Gods forward.

CHAPTER 17

The Fiery Furnace

THE FIRE OF the furnace leapt nearly fifteen feet into the air. To the right of the furnace stood the idol of the god Marduk. In the courtyard before the Ishtar Gate, the people danced and sang as the musicians played their instruments. Looking down on the crowd from atop a raised platform built for the occasion, Nebuchadnezzar sat with his new bride on their couches. To the king's right, Haman had taken his place. It was his show to preside over, and while he did not have Daniel in his clutches, the Chief Priest took satisfaction in knowing Daniel's top three advisors would soon depart this world.

At the king's command, the furnace had been stoked to an unbearable level for those standing anywhere near it. Their wrists bound, ankle shackles linked the three Hebrews together as they were dragged through the Ishtar gate into Nebuchadnezzar's presence. Though they offered no resistance, six soldiers beat them and picked them up to cast them into the furnace. As one, the three were thrown into the flames. Like the mouth of a hungry animal, the fire roared, snapping out a tongue of flame. Two of the soldiers were caught by the fiery eruption, and cried out in agony. Though more soldiers attempted to extinguish their comrades, the two were burned beyond recognition or hope of survival.

The music stopped. The dancers ceased their whirling to watch the death of the two soldiers. A piercing scream from Nebuchadnezzar's bride jerked the Chaldeans' attention back to the furnace, as she grabbed the king and pointed in its direction.

"Haman!" Nebuchadnezzar said, his breath coming in ragged gasps. "Were not three men thrown into the furnace?"

Unable to take his eyes from the furnace and its contents, Haman answered weakly. "Yes, O King."

"By the gods, I see four men loosed and walking about - and the appearance of the fourth is like a son of the gods!" The king looked around him at his people; saw the panic in their eyes. At the moment that Marduk's power should be celebrated, the Hebrews instead were making a mockery of his god. If he did not act quickly, the panic hiding behind the onlookers' eyes would quickly turn into a riot. Nebuchadnezzar walked down from the raised platform in the direction of the furnace, and called for the three to come out. All of the courtesans gathered 'round the three Hebrews as they emerged from the fire unharmed. Not only had they not been harmed by the blaze, but their clothing was untouched - not even smelling of smoke! Yet their bindings were gone, burned off their wrists and ankles.

Nebuchadnezzar looked around him. Saw the fear in the faces of his people. Heard murmuring. Haman interrupted his thoughts and whispered to him: "My King! You must bless these three and demonstrate your power in this situation."

Nodding to acknowledge Haman's advice, Nebuchadnezzar stood, cleared his voice, and said: "Praise to the God of Shadrach, Meshach, and Abednego! He sent his angel to rescue his servants who trusted in him. They defied the king's command and were willing to die rather than serve or worship any god except their own God. Therefore, I make this decree: If any people, whatever their race or nation or language, speak a word against the God of Shadrach, Meshach, and Abednego, they will be torn limb from limb, and their houses will be turned into heaps of rubble. There is no other god who can rescue like this! The three of you are free to go."

With that, Nebuchadnezzar sat down and watched as the three

Hebrews left his presence. Once they had left, the king grabbed Haman by the shoulders, a look of fear and desperation in his eyes. "Now, for the first time, I fear Daniel and those whom he has chosen as his closest advisors. In the face of our most sacred occasion, his God has made a mockery of us. We must go and talk. I need your help in knowing what to do."

Haman was taken aback by Nebuchadnezzar's reaction. Surviving the fire had been a cheap magician's trick. He didn't know how the three Hebrews had done it. That did not matter. What mattered was that they find a way to seize this opportunity to glorify Nebuchadnezzar, demonstrating that the Hebrews were still servants of Marduk and the other gods of Babylon.

Now, perhaps, he would have a chance to enlist the king's aide in disposing of Daniel. Yes! There was still hope that he could eliminate the one man who stood in his way. He smiled at the King, and put his arm around Nebuchadnezzar's shoulder. Haman knew just what to do.

"Come, Nebuchadnezzar, let us go speak in private. I have a plan."

Daniel loosened his traveling cloak as the midmorning sun warmed his body. Looking back over his shoulder, he saw a mist still clinging to the mountains from which they had just descended. In a few hours he and his escort would reach the trade route that, in a day's ride, would bring them to Babylon. Two of the ten soldiers escorting him had ridden on ahead to intercept a large caravan they had seen headed their way to learn who they were. This close to Babylon, it was unlikely they would pose a threat, but his protectors wished to take no chances.

Daniel rode in silence, paying little attention to those around him, even Ezekiel, who had joined him at the last minute as they departed Babylon. Daniel had seen his old friend amongst the newly arriving exiles and had taken Ezekiel with him to pray and fast in the foothills of the Zagros mountains. Daniel's heart had rejoiced to again see his friend, to learn of his family and his people. Yet this had not been a time set aside for celebration, but for fasting, prayer and intercession. Last night, those prayers had culminated in a vision as clear as the one he had had the night he "saw" Nebuchadnezzar's dream.

And it had terrified him. It was as though he had been there, in person, walking around in a fire which burned hotter than the sun itself. In that fire with him had been Shadrach, Abednego and Meshach. As hot as the flames had been, they had not been consumed by the blaze. The vision had ended when the three exited the furnace, and Haman had left with Nebuchadnezzar to discuss the meaning of it all. The look on the king's face showed that he was clearly afraid. Up until now, Daniel had seen Nebuchadnezzar as one who would lend his protection to Daniel and his people. Now, he was not so sure. For the first time in four days, Daniel turned to his friend to share what was in his heart.

"Ezekiel, I am convinced God has led our people into exile as a way to refine us, as a way to prepare us for something. With the exception of Josiah, our kings have led us further and further astray. By being taken into exile in Babylon, we have been forced to look inward and examine our hearts, to renew our spirits. I want to accomplish that task, and am convinced you will play a key role in that endeavor."

"But, Ezekiel, I fear the implications of my vision. The Feast of Akitu is a time when the King of Babylon takes on the powers of Marduk. Nebuchadnezzar could easily view what happened last night as a terrible insult to his god. If that happens, what is to prevent him from taking revenge on our people? Should my fears come true, whatever dreams the Lord has in mind for us will die unborn."

"But what of the scrolls, Daniel? You have been here nearly five years and have had time to study them. You told me yourself Nebuchadnezzar has made available to you his magicians, mathematicians and astronomers. Have you been able to learn anything?" Ezekiel asked.

The scroll of Isaiah made mention of a conqueror who was to come, one called Cyrus. Without giving voice to the prophecy, Daniel silently recalled what Isaiah had written:

"Thus says the Lord to Cyrus His anointed: God shall empower his right hand and he shall crush the strength of mighty kings. God shall open the gates of Babylon to you; I will shatter the doors of bronze, and cut through their iron bars. And I will give you the treasures of darkness, and hidden wealth of secret places, in order that you may know it is I, The Lord, the God of Israel, who calls you by name."

But there was a darker secret which revealed a prophecy that Daniel could not bring himself to share with his friend. It was a prophecy of judgment which revealed not only that the temple would be destroyed, but also the exact date on which that event would take place. The thought that these things would happen was too terrifying to think about, let alone discuss with Ezekiel.

> **Isaiah's Prophecy of Cyrus the Great**
>
> *"Thus says the Lord to Cyrus His anointed: God shall empower his right hand and he shall crush the strength of mighty kings. God shall open the gates of Babylon to you."*
>
> To learn more about Isaiah's prophecy, read Isaiah chapters 44 and 45. What might Daniel's "darker secret" be?

"Yes, there are some things that I have learned, still other things that remain hazy to me. I cannot discuss them now, but know this: My vision of last night portends events far beyond what we can now imagine. We must leave it in God's hands, knowing He will provide a shepherd who will restore our people at the right time."

Their conversation was interrupted by one of their Babylonian escorts, who called for the party to halt. Out of the west, two horsemen galloped toward them - the scouts who had been sent out earlier to investigate the approaching caravan. The horses, snorting and shaking their heads, were reined in by their riders. Before the steeds settled down, the two warriors dismounted and approached, saluting their captain. "Give me your report!," he commanded.

"Lord Naaman himself leads the troop which even now comes our way. He orders us to join him in his triumphant return to Babylon." Turning to Daniel, the scout added, "Lord Naaman expresses his good wishes to you and eagerly anticipates your joining his command."

As their party resumed its trek towards Babylon with the intent of joining up with Naaman, Ezekiel turned to Daniel and said, "Now we shall have a rare opportunity to learn what he thinks of Judah's new king - and what relationship our people can expect to enjoy with Babylon."

Daniel nodded his head, and said a prayer for his people.

No matter how many times Naaman returned to Babylon, its beauty never ceased to amaze him. Now within the inner wall, the city gates loomed large and magnificent against a deep blue sky. But for all its beauty and the anticipation of his return to her ramparts, Naaman could not put the worries that crowded his thoughts out of his head.

Last night at camp, Daniel had told him all that had transpired - of Timnah's coming to warn him of Haman's treachery, of how she had urged him to use the excuse of going into the mountains to pray for Nebuchadnezzar as a ruse to get him out of the city. And Daniel had told him of the vision he had had of his friends in a fiery furnace. Naaman had paid little attention to the story, but now he was not so sure.

Arriving as they had on the day after the feast of Akitu, the city stood in eerie silence, the residents for the most part sleeping off the effects of the seven day-long festivities. As a result, the turnout to welcome Naaman's return was smaller than usual. Only a ceremonial guard awaited them. What struck Naaman as extremely odd was the way they acted toward Daniel, the way they looked - No! Did not look at him, but rather averted their eyes and kept their heads bowed in his presence. Something had happened, but what?

"You, there," Naaman said to the sergeant in charge of the ceremonial guard sent to welcome them home. "Where is King Nebuchadnezzar?"

"He is in counsel with Haman the High Priest. They are discussing what to do regarding the omen which was seen during the great feast."

"What omen?" Naaman asked, thinking about the vision which Daniel had described to him. The guard stole a quick glance at Daniel, clearly fearful of answering in the presence of the Hebrew holy man.

"A great and awesome event occurred while you were gone, Lord Naaman. It is that about which they speak. I have been ordered to escort you to the King," the sergeant hesitated before proceeding, afraid to look at, let alone speak to Daniel. "King Nebuchadnezzar wishes for the Great Belteshazzar to await him at the temple of Etemenanki. He will greet you there, and thanks you for your prayers and fasting on his behalf."

Naaman looked at Daniel. "Something has happened because of your vision, Daniel, which has frightened my people terribly. Go and pray to your god for mercy, for I fear an ill wind blows a storm which will engulf us. I will go and see what has transpired."

"I have no power to see my future, or yours, Naaman, but of this I am certain," said Daniel. "No harm will befall me. Therefore, do not fear for my sake. Rather, think about what we have spoken in the past. Our God has brought us to Babylon to be cleansed of our sins. What is happening now is part of that process." Daniel turned aside, and accompanied by Ezekiel and his original escort, proceeded to the temple of Etemenanki to pray.

Naaman left the rest of his command in the care of his aide-de-camp and allowed the sergeant to lead him to the Court of Nebuchadnezzar. He thought back to that first time when he had met Daniel and spoken to him; how Daniel had said his God had ordained they would be taken into captivity for seventy years as a punishment for their sins. Naaman had from the beginning feared that the policy of bringing different conquered peoples to Babylon would affect his people. Though he liked and respected Daniel, Naaman had increasingly come to fear the power the Hebrews had to influence his own people. And he knew that part of his fear was based on the fact that he was himself drawn to the idea that only one god, not dozens, held the fate of the world in his hands.

Little did he know that soon, Haman would use Daniel's obedience to pray to his God to spring a trap which would lead to the young Hebrew's doom.

CHAPTER **18**

Haman Makes his Plans

HE RED STAR in Orion's belt twinkled as a ruby in the clear night sky.

As Haman looked out his window at the stars above, he savored the sense of elation which coursed through his veins. Nebuchadnezzar had heard and agreed to his plan - one which would acknowledge the events of the other evening, but which would position the Hebrew god as being wholly subservient to Marduk. And they owed it all to Daniel's teacher, this so-called prophet named Jeremiah.

Neither Haman nor Nebuchadnezzar could allow the escape of the three Hebrews from the fiery furnace to go without explanation. So, Haman had devised a scheme which allowed Nebuchadnezzar to not only take credit for their survival, but claim that the king had himself been the agent of their escape from the furnace. Haman had written a decree, which Nebuchadnezzar had signed and was now being distributed throughout the kingdom. For perhaps the twentieth time, Haman again read the parchment containing the decree as he drained his wine goblet.

The prophet Jeremiah has written the exiles in Babylon, saying: "Build houses and settle down. Marry, have sons and daughters. Increase in numbers, do not decrease. Also, seek the peace and prosperity of the city of Babylon, praying to the Lord for it, because if Babylon prospers, you too will prosper. The

God of Israel has appointed Nebuchadnezzar, King of Babylon, as his servant - to bring salvation to your people. He is the Messiah of the Hebrews."

Yet, some of the Hebrews have doubted the will of their god, so Nebuchadnezzar put you to the test. Of all the Hebrews, only Meshach, Shadrach and Abednego passed that test - to trust in the God of Israel, who has sent you to Babylon to serve Nebuchadnezzar. Praise be to the God of Meshach, Shadrach and Abednego, who has sent his angel and rescued his servants! They trusted in Him, and did not worship the gods of the Babylonians. With the blessing of Marduk, their god saved them from the fiery furnace, so that the Hebrews would honor his command to dwell in Babylon and serve her king. For, how else could the god of Meshach, Shadrach and Abednego save them if it were not the will of Marduk? Therefore, because of their faithfulness, these three will be given positions of power in the Kingdom of Babylon.

Furthermore, the God of Israel will be given a place of honor with the Gods of Babylon, and sit at Markduk's right hand. From this day forward, to commemorate his inclusion into the House of the Gods, his name shall be called Beelzebub.

Haman laughed as he read that last line, for in the language of the Hebrews, the name Beelzebub meant "Lord of the flies." The effect would not be lost on his people - which both he and the king agreed was needed to restore their faith in the gods of Babylon after what had happened. Haman looked up again at the red star in Orion's belt. He knew there was no explanation for what had happened the other night. But, rather than deny that it had happened, they would embrace it - claiming that it had been the will of Marduk all along - and that the god of the Hebrews would join the Pantheon of Babylonian gods pledged to serve Marduk. As the people on earth were assimilated by their Chaldean masters, so too their god would be assimilated by the gods of this land. It was a simple solution to a complex problem.

Haman heard the woman approach behind him, felt her wrap her arms around his chest.

"I grew tired of waiting for you to come back. Still thinking about your triumph from earlier today, eh my Lord?" Timnah asked.

"Yes," Haman answered, still looking up at the stars. "And what was best was Daniel's reaction to the good news." Haman savored the memory as he prepared to tell his mistress. "We summoned the Hebrew after Naaman gave his report. Nebuchadnezzar announced that the god of the Hebrews would henceforth be called Beelzebub, and added to the Pantheon of idols to be celebrated in the future New Year's celebrations. Even now, the goldsmiths have been commissioned to form idols for purchase by the people - especially the Hebrews living in Babylon.

"But why wouldn't Daniel see that as a good thing?," asked Timnah, slowly caressing the Chief Priest.

"Because they refuse to make idols of their God - in fact, their religion forbids it. Daniel has said many times that his god is 'The One True God.' He realizes that by making his God one of the Babylonian Pantheon, the religion of his people will be compromised. Not only that, but as the greater has the power to change the name of the lesser, Marduk is elevated over the god of the Hebrews whose name is now Beelzebub, the Lord of the Flies. In a generation, they will lose their distinctiveness, and be of no trouble to anyone."

"And now that Daniel has been discredited before the eyes of the king, what do you intend to do?" she asked, turning the man around to look into her eyes.

"Nebuchadnezzar fears the power of Daniel. He has appointed the Hebrew to a position of power, and cannot undo that. But, at a time of my choosing, he will take an action which will force Daniel to defy a royal command, and thus forfeit his life. For now, that is all I can say, as I must take my leave. I have much to do today." Haman kissed her on the cheek and turned to leave. But as he did so, he resolved to be much less free with the information he shared with the Queen of Ashkelon, for one question still ate at him - had Daniel been forewarned of the plan to force the Hebrews to bow down to Nebuchadnezzar? Daniel's sudden appearance with an excuse to be out of the city during the New Year's celebration had been far too convenient. If Daniel had been alerted by someone, Timnah's name would lead a short list of suspects.

He would have to satisfy his suspicions, and if it proved that she had betrayed him, take the steps necessary to ensure her future silence.

CHAPTER 19

Thermostats and Governors

ISAIAH LOOKED AT the easel where Grandpa had hung pictures of all the different Babylonian gods. He remembered the part of the story where, after the flood, they descended like flies to eat the offerings that the one guy – what had Grandpa said his name was? Ut … Ut … Utnapishtim! The offerings that Utnapishtim and his family made. In return, the Babylonian gods promised to never again destroy mankind because they needed humans to feed them.

But God – the prophet Daniel's God – the God who was the Father of Jesus – was a kind and loving God. When Noah had offered a sacrifice, God had put a rainbow in the sky as a promise to never again try to destroy mankind by a flood.

Deep down inside, Isaiah knew that Grandpa was getting ready to come to the "grand finale," a term he'd recently learned meant the dramatic end of a story. Nebuchadnezzar had wanted everyone to pray to his gods. But Daniel and his friends would only pray to the real God. Somehow, the power to tell people who they could and could not pray to was a very important power.

It was as if King Nebuchadnezzar and Haman couldn't tell Daniel and his friends what to do because they only listened to God. So, the only way to get everyone to do what King Nebuchadnezzar and the Chief Priest Haman wanted them to do was to worship THEIR gods instead of the ONE TRUE God.

This was something he had to ask Grandpa about.

"Grandpa, I have a question."

"Good, because I need a break before we finish the story, Isaiah!" replied Grandpa as he sat down. They both looked around and saw that Nai Nai, Nadia and Josiah had all fallen asleep, so Grandpa whispered; "Let's go to the kitchen and get a Coke, and you can ask me your question there and we won't wake everyone else up."

Sitting at the kitchen table, with the caffeine jolt from the Coke helping to bring his mind into focus, Isaiah asked his question.

"Grandpa," he began, "I've been thinking about why the ancients had all those gods. It seems to me that when you tell people you've got lots of gods to obey, then all the people in the government need to come up with lots of rules to make sure the people obey what the rulers say the gods want them to do."

Isaiah took another sip of his Coke, and then continued. "Today, we don't have lots of gods, but we do have lots of rulers - politicians. So, if you want to make people do what you want them to do, then instead of having people believe in lots of idols, you need the people to believe in lots of rulers. So, whether it's Babylon with lots of idols, or our world today with lots of rulers, if people believe in only one God, then they are less likely to do the things the rulers say when they tell the people to do something that is against what God says."

Isaiah paused, looked down at his Coke, and then back up at his grandfather. Then, with a confused look on his face, he said: "Does that make sense? Am I right, Grandpa?"

Grandpa got up from his chair and motioned for Isaiah to do the same. They walked quietly from the kitchen, past the Sunroom where everyone was sleeping, to the hallway leading to the bedrooms. When they got to where he wanted them to go, Grandpa stopped, turned on the light, and pointed to the object he wanted to show Isaiah.

"Isaiah, this is called a thermostat. I set the temperature where I want it to be, and then our heating and cooling system keeps the temperature of the house where I set it to be. Have you ever thought about how a thermostat does that?"

Isaiah shook his head no. "Nope, but I bet you're going to tell me! Does this have something to do with having politicians who are rulers telling us what to do?"

Grandpa smiled a great big smile. "Do you know what the top politician of a state's title is, Isaiah?"

"Ah, Governor?"

"Absolutely!" replied Grandpa. "Now, there is a little device inside the thermostat that measures the temperature and tells the heating system to turn on and off to keep the temperature of the house where it needs to be. Want to guess what it's called?"

"Ah, a Governor?" Isaiah said tentatively. When Grandpa nodded his head, Isaiah added, "Grandpa, are you telling me that we have politicians in all the houses telling the house what the temperature should be?"

"Not quite, silly boy!" Grandpa said with big smile. "But the governor inside the thermostat is like the Holy Spirit of God inside your heart. When you get too far away from doing what God wants you to do, He speaks to you through your conscience and tells you to adjust your behavior, to stop doing what is wrong, and start doing what is right. So, Isaiah, what you said about Christians being reluctant to do things they know in their hearts is wrong, even if a ruler tells them to do it, is correct."

Isaiah thought about that for a moment, and then said, "So when the prophet Daniel and his friends were told to bow down to idols, or to eat food sacrificed to idols, or other things they knew were against God's law, they said 'no'. But they also tried to find a way to say 'no' so that they could present the rulers with a reasonable alternative so everyone could come out with a win-win. Is that right?"

"By Jove, my boy, I do believe you've got it!" Grandpa said with his best attempt at a British accent.

"But Grandpa," continued Isaiah, "what happens when the ruler doesn't accept the alternative? Then what do you do?"

"Well, Isaiah, as you heard in the story, God's people must be willing to pay the price when they disobey the rulers. Do you remember when King Nebuchadnezzar wanted Daniel's three friends to bow down?"

"They said no, didn't they?"

"Yes, that's right. Here's what Shadrach said – you'll find it in the Bible, Daniel 3:18. Here's what God's word says:

"Our God, whom we serve, is able to deliver us from the furnace you have prepared. But even if He chooses not to do so, Oh King, know that we can never bow down and serve any image of any god."

Grandpa looked at his grandson and said: "Sometimes, for His own glory, God rescues us from bad things. And sometimes, even though we may not like it or don't understand why, God calls people home to Heaven, but does not rescue them from their own 'fiery furnace.' We never know exactly why, even though it can make us very sad."

Isaiah looked down and nodded, and then said. "It's sort of like when my dog, Princess, got hit by a car. She was getting ready to have puppies. I prayed so hard that she would live, but that just wasn't to be."

Grandpa patted Isaiah on the shoulder, and remembered the time they'd lost their pet.

Isaiah took a deep breath, then looked back up. "Auntie Dr. Sarah said you'd tell us about a law that got passed in Babylon that made it illegal to pray to God. I'll bet Daniel would have obeyed the 'governor' inside his heart and prayed anyway. Am I right?"

"Well, Isaiah, for the answer to that, let's go back to the kitchen and I'll finish the story. We'll let everyone else sleep." With that, Daniel went to the kitchen, while Grandpa went quietly back into the Sunroom to retrieve his special book.

CHAPTER 20

Naaman Is Ambushed

Though they were no longer in the Sunroom, Grandpa resumed his stance, standing over his special book, The Chronicles of Belteshazzar. Turning to the next part of the story, he began to read:

In the ninth year of the Reign of Nebuchadnezzar, the fifth year of the reign of Zedekiah in Jerusalem, the treachery of Haman was revealed. Daniel was thrown into the lions' den, but the God of Daniel thwarted the schemes of the High Priest of Babylon. Over two hundred of Haman's supporters and their families were eventually captured and fed to the lions. A small civil war ensued in Babylon as the last of his allies were rooted out and destroyed. News of the resulting furor traveled to Jerusalem, where the mad prophets used it as an excuse for Judah to join with other nations in rebellion against Babylon and prophecy the imminent return of the exiles. The prophet Jeremiah was himself taken prisoner. Though not swift, the response by Babylon, when it did come, was more than sure.

Chronicles of Belteshazzar

The moment of truth had come. Haman stepped into the Great Hall and awaited the Sergeant of Arms to announce his presence.

Now, at the end of the Festival of Bel, the harvest festival, everything was in place to allow Haman's plans to come to full fruition.

"Haman, High Priest of the Realm of Babylon!" The gatekeeper formally announced Haman's arrival. Haman's eyes locked with Nebuchadnezzar's, and he bowed his head. Nebuchadnezzar had been desperate to find a means to explain the survival of the three Hebrews in the fiery furnace. Haman had seized that opportunity which would not only make Nebuchadnezzar beholden to him, and destroy Daniel, but also increase his own power. The first part of the plan had now been accomplished, with the completion of the new temple containing the idol for the Hebrews to worship. Haman not only enriched himself from the new revenue source of the temple sacrifices, but used the food sacrifices to secretly reward his supporters. The added wealth and renewed loyalty of his own followers would strengthen Haman's hand when the time came to implement his own private agenda.

Today, he would set in motion the second part of his plan, which months ago he had described to Nebuchadnezzar in great detail. Today, he would propose an ordinance, which Nebuchadnezzar would approve, that would lead to Daniel's death. With Daniel out of the way, the king would have unwittingly removed the one obstacle preventing Haman's agents from stirring up the tensions among the native Babylonians and the exile groups. Haman would use the resulting unrest to execute the third part of his plan - the crowning of himself as king of Babylon.

"Hail, Haman, and welcome to our court!" Nebuchadnezzar responded to Haman's announcement.

"Oh King, may you live forever!" Haman replied, and approached Nebuchadnezzar's throne. Haman glanced around the room, and was pleased to see that all of the provincial governors were present. Haman had chosen this day carefully, because he knew that they would be in the city for the festival. Haman had worked to secure their agreement with the proclamation he held in his hand. Like himself, they too chafed at the idea that a foreigner had risen to such a prominent position in the Babylonian government. Indeed, in their private meetings, Nebuchadnezzar had urged that the decree come from all of the governmental officials. "How would I be able to refuse an honor which all of my governors wished to bestow on me?" Nebuchadnezzar had commented to Haman in mock humility during those meetings. Yes, the stage was set and awaited only Haman's request to trigger the drama which was about to unfold.

"Great Nebuchadnezzar! We have celebrated the Festival of Bel, and have praised the gods for the bounty with which they have blessed us. But it is you, oh King, who has established our kingdom and have provided prosperity so that we might serve the gods. Therefore, all the governors, counselors, princes and captains have consulted together to establish this royal statute: That whosoever shall ask a petition from any of the gods for the next 30 days shall be cast into the den of lions, save this: If any man makes his petition of you, oh King, he shall live and not be cast into the lions' den. Furthermore, let the people bring their sacrifices and petitions of you to the new Temple of Beelzebub in honor of your latest work honoring the gods. Therefore, for the next month, the people shall worship only Nebuchadnezzar, protector of the Gods of Babylon."

Haman approached Nebuchadnezzar's seat and unrolled the small scroll containing the decree. A scribe came forward to accept the document and hand it to the king. Taking the stylus in hand, he looked around the room. As Haman had planned, Daniel was not present. His gaze fell upon the place where Naaman would have been, vacant because of a false emergency Haman had arranged that required the Captain of the Guard's attention. Looking into the King's eyes, Haman watched as Nebuchadnezzar reached first for the decree, and then for the stylus in order to sign the document.

Smiling, Nebuchadnezzar said, "So shall it be written, so shall it be done. By my hand I establish this decree which not even I can revoke."

Haman smiled as the king signed the decree, going over in his mind how to take Daniel. A creature of habit, the wizard prayed to his god three times daily. Indeed, Haman had chosen this hour to request the decree, knowing that Daniel would be away from the court consumed by the worship of his pitiful god. Within twenty-four hours, news of the proclamation would have spread throughout the city. By morning, his agents would apprehend Daniel for disobeying the ordinance. That would be the end of his enemy.

Followed by four of his guards, Naaman set a swift and steady pace towards Etemenanki, where Daniel had his prayer chamber. Soon after the Ziggurat had been completed, Daniel had moved his quarters to the temple for the sake of convenience in praying to his God. Daniel would be arising in about a half-hour to go and make his morning prayers, so Naaman didn't have much time to prevent his friend from violating the decree which Nebuchadnezzar had issued.

Not for the first time, Naaman asked himself why he had not been made aware of the decree sooner. Timnah had come looking for him, but he had been in another part of the city when she had arrived. The servant with whom she had left the message had failed to convey it to him, when he had finally come home to retire for the night. Had he not awakened from a fitful sleep and learned of Timnah's attempt to reach him from one of the other servants, he would have had no chance to warn Daniel. As it was, Naaman could not be certain that Haman's henchmen did not already lay in wait, hoping to catch Daniel violating Nebuchadnezzar's decree.

Rounding a corner, Naaman could see the outline of the ziggurat of Etemenanki in the pre-dawn light. Daniel's quarters were on the second level of the edifice, from where he would have to climb the stairs to reach the prayer chamber on the sixth level - though Daniel sometimes chose to pray within his quarters. If he couldn't persuade Daniel to suspend his prayer ritual, Naaman resolved to use force, at least on this occasion, to achieve his goal. It was a dangerous game he was playing, and right now, Naaman was reacting to circumstances. Though he longed for the chance to think through this series of events, it was an opportunity that would elude him.

Absorbed in his thoughts, Naaman failed to notice the beggar sitting against the building he had just rounded, asleep with a cloak pulled over his head. Naaman and his men neared the base of the Ziggurat and began to make their way toward the wide marble staircase of the edifice. A few feet from the staircase, a second beggar appeared in their path. Bent over and leaning on a staff, the man lifted his cup, saying "Alms, alms for the poor. Surely my lord can turn aside and help an old cripple forsaken by the gods?"

"Out of my way, old man," Naaman said, pushing the outstretched hand away and continuing to move past him. Dimly in the subconscious reaches of his brain, Naaman registered a foreign accent in the beggar's voice, one hard to place. In the split second of hesitation of noting something amiss and reacting to it, the beggar pivoted in a three hundred sixty-degree turn, whipping the staff around him in an arch aimed at Naaman's knees. Unable to avoid the blow, the staff hit him in the calf muscles. With the deftness of one accustomed to wielding the staff, Naaman's attacker - he was clearly no mere beggar - lifted his feet out from under him. Gritting his teeth as the pain from the blow shot through his legs, Naaman slapped his forearms to the ground, breaking his fall as he landed on his back.

With no time to recover, Naaman saw his assailant draw a sword and prepare to bring it down with a powerful two-handed blow to his head. Naaman rolled toward the man, crashing into his shins and causing him to tumble forward. Painfully, Naaman gained his footing and, drawing his sword, watched his opponent recover from his tumble and come to his feet, sword pointed at Naaman.

Stealing a quick look at the scene around him, Naaman saw one of his men down, another wounded and realized they had walked into a trap. These were no homeless beggars, but skilled warriors bent on preventing Naaman and his men from reaching Daniel! Naaman let out a war cry and charged the assassin. Feinting with a two-handed sword thrust at the enemy, Naaman then swiftly pivoted clockwise on his left foot, bringing his sword in a curving upward arch to try to slip below the man's defenses. But just as quickly, the warrior parried his blow and countered with one of his own, grazing Naaman's momentarily exposed midsection. In that instant, Naaman realized that his opponent, his equal in physical stature, was clearly as skilled as himself - perhaps more so. As their swords met and sparks flew, Naaman looked into the dark eyes of his enemy, and putting the man's accent together with his features, snarled, "You are a dead man, you Greek dog!" Letting go of his blade with his left hand, Naaman struck a blow to the man's chin, rocking him backwards.

But before Naaman could follow up his momentary advantage, he was felled by a blow to his head. His helmet went rolling as Naaman managed to break his fall with both hands.

"Guards coming! Troas, we must leave *now!*" A voice said from somewhere. Three sets of footsteps retreated from the scene, leaving Naaman dazed. Shaking his head to fend off unconsciousness, Naaman looked around to see two of his men badly wounded the other two not moving and presumably dead. A fifth man lay still, presumably one of the attackers who had ambushed them.

> **Troas the Greek Mercenary**
>
> The story line of Daniel in Babylon was first written as part of a longer novel, **The Brotherhood of the Scroll**. In that novel, the Greek mercenary Troas plays a much greater role. During this time period, the Egyptians hired Greek mercenaries to supplement their army. Visit www.wisejargon.com/ brotherhood to learn more about the original novel.

Turning his head, Naaman saw a small troop of soldiers with the emblem of Haman's personal bodyguard approach. Two of their number broke rank to attend to Naaman and his surviving men. The rest proceeded to mount the steps of Etemenanki. As Naaman slipped into unconsciousness, he was vaguely aware that he had failed to protect Daniel.

CHAPTER 21

Daniel Is Thrown to the Lions

NAAMAN, HIS HEAD throbbing, walked with Daniel and his captors as they neared Nebuchadnezzar's palace. He had described his attackers to those in his command who had come to him at once upon hearing of the attack. At the very end, someone had called out to the man who had attacked him – calling him "Troas." Was he their leader? Naaman's first thought had been that the attackers were in Haman's pay, but then why had the Priest's guards come to his rescue? No, while the Greek attackers seemed to be in league with Haman, it could not be. The only other alternative was that they were here for their own reasons, which included wishing to see Daniel taken prisoner. Naaman would have to get to the bottom of this mystery, but his more immediate concern was Daniel's imminent trial and sentencing. Naaman could not be seen attempting to aid Daniel in his defiance of the king's decree, but how could he save his friend? If only Daniel had had the common sense to suspend his religious practices, at least for a time!

Arriving at the Court of Nebuchadnezzar, they waited for the King to call for them.. After nearly an hour, Naaman followed Daniel and his captors into the Great Hall to find Haman already there. The Chief Priest began the proceedings and read off the charges against Daniel.

"Daniel, a Hebrew captive who has come to be known as Belteshazzar; appointed the Chief Scribe, has been granted the privilege of serving in your court. Yet, today, this same person was found in flagrant disregard of one of our commandments. Did you not, King Nebuchadnezzar, establish a decree that for the next thirty days, no man could make any supplication to or request of the gods, save to your divine self?"

"I did so command," Nebuchadnezzar said, looking down at the floor instead of at Daniel.

Haman continued to press his case. "This Hebrew, Daniel, was caught this morning - the very day after your decree was issued - making such supplication. Though he has been appointed to high office, he must face the full penalty of our laws - he must be cast into the lions' den. To allow him to escape the King's law would invite anyone to believe themselves above the laws of our people!"

Naaman watched the eyebrows of Nebuchadnezzar furrow as he listened to Haman's request. Could the king be experiencing second thoughts now that his destiny had been forced upon him? Torn between the urge to speak out in Daniel's defense and his fear of choosing the losing side in this confrontation, Timnah's warning came back to strike him like a dagger. He could not rise to Daniel's defense without appearing to be a traitor and thereby jeopardizing his own position.

While Naaman stood frozen by indecision, Nebuchadnezzar finally answered Haman. "It is as you say. I have made the decree, and no man may break it under penalty of death. At sunset, Daniel is to be cast into the den of lions where he shall remain until sunrise tomorrow. Belteshazzar," Nebuchadnezzar said to Daniel, using his Babylonian name one last time, "You have been a trusted servant. If you are blameless in this case, may your god whom you worship continually save you." Nebuchadnezzar rose from his throne and retreated down the hallway leading to his private chambers.

Naaman shook his head, suddenly realizing how foolish he had been. Nebuchadnezzar had spoken to Daniel in a mocking tone - he had not meant any of these words. Timnah had been right; Naaman should never have become as closely associated with Daniel as he had. Perhaps the gods had been smiling on him after all for stopping him from confronting Daniel this morning! Had he been found with Daniel, Haman would no doubt have found a way to implicate him in Daniel's crime.

Naaman's only desire was to leave the palace. In the morning, he would go to see whether Daniel lived or died. For now, he simply wanted to escape his own sense of shame and guilt.

Daniel awoke, slowly, shaking off the effects of a deep sleep. His semiconscious mind still held the visions he had seen this night: The sight of the Temple of Beelzebub and the priests bringing grain and animal sacrifices into the inner sanctuary. Each morning, the sacrifices had vanished when the chamber maids came to clean the holy places. In his dream, Daniel had seen people ascending and descending a staircase hidden behind the idol of Beelzebub. From this vision, Daniel knew how Haman was using the temple to use the sacrifices to line his own pockets and reward his supporters with food and gold. Haman had intended the temple as an insult to his God – calling it a name that meant "Lord of the Flies." But Haman would discover that it would spell his doom.

He remembered little of his entrance into the cave - only that he had been given a small torch which soon went out. Now, as he became fully awake, Daniel could hear the deep, steady breathing of the bodies around him - smelled their odors. Then Daniel remembered where he was! Not merely in a cave, but a lions' den! Above him, the sound of voices filtered down. Moments later, a great stone was rolled away, and Daniel could look out of the cave to an overcast sky. As he stood up, the opening only two feet above his head, a voice called out:

"Daniel, are you alive? Was your god able to save you?" Laughter greeted this disembodied voice of - Nebuchadnezzar? Adrenaline pumping, Daniel crouched down, and then leaped for the opening. His hands grasping the edges of the aperture, others laid hold of him and pulled him up to safety. No sooner had he picked himself up and stood among the people surrounding the lair's opening than the lions below let out a collective, hideous roar.

Daniel grimaced from the deafening noise, then looked around him at the stunned crowd. Not only were Haman and the Babylonian governors present; all the leaders of the exile groups were there, even Timnah. Daniel caught sight of Ezekiel. Even he had the same awestruck look like the rest. Then it dawned on him - Haman had hoped to use this moment to demonstrate his power, but now, he tried to make himself as small as possible.

"Indeed, oh King, my God was able to rescue me. He sent His angel to shut the mouths of the lions, so that I would come to no harm, for I am innocent before my God and my King." Daniel saw no reason not to answer Nebuchadnezzar's question by stating the obvious.

The king was visibly shaken. When he had spoken earlier, asking Daniel if his god had been able to save him, he had done so in jest. Now, all he could do was attempt to recover his poise in front of all those who were there. "Of your innocence there can be no doubt. You are free, Belteshazzar, innocent of all you've been accused."

Daniel bowed to Nebuchadnezzar, and then, in a quiet voice so that it would not carry to those around him, he said, "While I was in the lions' den, my God caused me to fall into a deep sleep. While I slept, He showed me a vision which I ask the opportunity to impart to you and to Naaman, alone. It involves a traitor to the King. Will my Lord grant me this audience?"

Nebuchadnezzar's eyes narrowed at the word traitor. "Yes," he replied. "After you have fed and refreshed yourself, we shall have that audience."

In a small sitting room, a servant poured three cups of wine and left. As Nebuchadnezzar and Naaman entered the room, Daniel rose to greet them. Each took a cup of wine and sat down. "To your health. May your reign be long and glorious," said Daniel raising his cup in a toast to the king. Nebuchadnezzar smiled warily and the three took a sip from their cups. Having thus broken the ice, Daniel began to describe his vision.

"King Nebuchadnezzar, I know that in these last few months, you and I have grown distant. But I am not your enemy. We have known for some time who that enemy is, but lacked a way to prove it to you. Last night, in the lions' den, my God revealed to me the means by which to give you that proof."

"And just who is my enemy?" Nebuchadnezzar asked, leaning back, eyes boring holes in Daniel.

"Haman, my Lord," he answered after first looking over at Naaman.

"Is this true? That you have suspected Haman of treason for some time?" Nebuchadnezzar said, turning to Naaman.

"Yes, my Lord," the Captain of the Guard replied.

"What is your evidence?" Nebuchadnezzar asked.

"As you may know, my King, each evening the sacrifices are brought to the new Temple of Beelzebub, and each morning, instead of being available for disbursement to the priests and the king's servants, the food sacrifices have vanished, ..." Daniel began.

"But is that not because your god is a hungry one?" interrupted Nebuchadnezzar.

Daniel shook his head no. "Despite what you may have been told, that is <u>not</u> my god - it is an abomination to my people! No, what Haman has done is to build a secret passageway behind the idol. At night, after the evening sacrifices, his people come in and take the food offerings. And, if you have noticed, they have also begun to ask the people for offerings of gold and silver."

"Haman began to demand such offerings at the same time you signed the decree requiring all prayers be made to you at the Temple of Beelzebub," Naaman interjected.

"Why was I not told of this!" Nebuchadnezzar demanded, leaning forward in his chair.

"Because, my Lord, Haman seeks your throne. He has long wished to stir up the passions of the exile groups against one another, as well as those of your own people, to create civil unrest, even riots. By causing panic in the streets, Haman would then orchestrate a coup, focusing the anger of the people on you. The people would then entrust their loyalty to him as the only person who could 'save' the kingdom from anarchy."

"I have a witness who can testify that it was Haman who was behind the attempt to assassinate Belteshazzar last year," Naaman interjected. "I have not sought to bring this evidence forward until now because I needed additional proof that would corroborate my witness's story."

"And who is this witness?" Nebuchadnezzar asked.

"Timnah, Queen of the Ashkelonites."

Nebuchadnezzar paused and thought about what Naaman had just said, then slowly nodded his head. "Yes, I can see why you would want additional evidence, since it was her people that attempted to kill Belteshazzar." Turning to Daniel, Nebuchadnezzar said, "Very well, then, what is your plan?"

For the next several minutes, Daniel explained how they could reveal what Haman was doing. The plans for their trap laid, Daniel and Naaman left to speak with Timnah. Tomorrow, she would be called upon to serve as a witness against Haman.

CHAPTER 22

Timnah Testifies Against Haman

A SERVANT HAD BROUGHT the letter to her this morning, sealed with the sign of Troas - an open eye in the middle of a pyramid. The words still blazed in her mind's eye: "Dear Timnah, I, Troas, still labor in the task about which I spoke with you and your father. I know you feel adrift here in Babylon, a pawn in a power struggle you cannot control. Please know that the plans to free your people proceed apace. I go now to Jerusalem where the league of nations in the Gaza Plain will formally adopt a treaty of alliance with Egypt. All that is needed is for the civil unrest planned by Haman to succeed. After Daniel's death, do what you can to ensure Nebuchadnezzar is distracted. We will do the rest to free your people and prepare for your return."

But Daniel had not died. Along with Naaman, he stood before her now to seek her help against Haman. She hated Haman, and knew that she could trust Naaman. Yet Troas needed Haman to succeed, for the sake of her people. What was she to do?

"Timnah, what is your answer? Now is the time to bring you forth as a witness against Haman." Naaman stood before her, hands on hips, the back of his head bandaged from the blow he had received the day before.

"But what if Nebuchadnezzar seeks to punish me for my role - worse, what if he should punish my people?" Timnah said, seeking to gain time to sort out her thoughts.

"Have no fear of that," Daniel said. "I forgave you long ago for your role in the attempt on my life. If I do not seek revenge, Nebuchadnezzar will not do so on my behalf." Drawing closer, Daniel placed his hands on her shoulders, and looked her straight in the eyes. Timnah tried to pull away, but he would not let her go.

"Listen to me," he said. "I know that you seek the release of your people from this place. As much as you hate Haman, you still cling to the hope that he will somehow aid you. You believe that the ensuing power struggle will divert Nebuchadnezzar's attention from your homeland and give them the chance they need to break his yoke. But you forget something," Daniel said, releasing her face and leaning back in his seat. "The same chaos that would ensue from a challenge from Haman would help my people. Do you not understand that if I believed Nebuchadnezzar could be defeated in this way, I would choose to help Haman myself?"

Timnah recoiled at his words. They made such sense - yet the thought had never entered her head. "Why don't you believe Haman can succeed?"

"Nebuchadnezzar had a dream which my God revealed to me. In that dream, Nebuchadnezzar established a great kingdom which will not be conquered during his lifetime - a long lifetime. Even if I wanted, I could not change the course of his empire. My God has established it. You, me, Naaman - as well as others - we are the instruments of His plan. But if we choose to act against His will, He will raise up others to take our places. He has called you to testify against Haman, but it is your choice to respond or not."

Timnah looked down at her hands. Despite the message from Troas, she knew Daniel was right. Suddenly, she closed her eyes and saw her father smiling at her, nodding his head. Timnah opened her eyes and looked up, first at Daniel, and then at Naaman. "If your plan is successful, and Haman is exposed, then I will testify against him in the morning."

"Good," Naaman said, slapping his hands together. "I leave now to set the trap. I will return for you in the morning." He smiled at Timnah, and left with Daniel close behind.

Timnah watched the door close behind the two, and suddenly felt the burden of revenge lift from her shoulders. For the first time since coming to Babylon, she was at peace with herself. She went to her bed chambers and retrieved the letter she had received from Troas. Reading it one more time, she went to a lamp and set the letter a blaze. As the flames consumed the letter, she resolved to serve her people as Daniel served his. She would not betray Troas, but she would seek to do his bidding no longer.

"Very well, I am here," Haman said, approaching Nebuchadnezzar without any sign of the customary deference shown the king. "But I protest you calling me to this temple to investigate the sacrifices being made to you. After all, was it not I who sought to honor you above all the gods of Babylon - even Marduk himself?"

"Yes, you did!" Nebuchadnezzar retorted. "Ever since, the offerings presented here have disappeared, and I have not received my portion of the tithe."

"A testimony to your true divinity, oh King. You should be overwhelmed by such tidings!" Haman replied.

"I think not," Nebuchadnezzar said in a short, hushed, even voice. "Come, we will enter this temple which you have built to honor the god of the Hebrews. Belteshazzar will lead the way." Nebuchadnezzar gestured for Daniel to enter the Temple of Beelzebub, while Haman, Nebuchadnezzar and Naaman followed. They were accompanied by several of Haman's personal guards, as well as men under Naaman's command.

As they entered the edifice, several guards stepped out of the shadows to bind Haman's men. Seeing what was happening, Haman turned to Naaman. "What is the meaning of this? Order your guards to release my men at once!"

Drawing his sword and holding its tip against the Chief Priest's throat, Naaman smiled and shook his head. "It is for your own protection, priest. Being true believers, they might wish to kill you for causing the sacrilege we are about to witness." Applying a momentary increase in pressure without drawing blood, Naaman removed his sword and grabbed a torch from its wall socket, ordering his guards to open the door to the inner sanctuary.

Inside the temple stood a gold statue of a man with a ram's head. Standing eight feet tall, the hands of the idol extended forward, palms up, as if to receive a sacrifice. Daniel took the lead as they proceeded closer to the idol. Holding out his hand to indicate they should stay where they were, he stopped and pointed to the floor stones immediately in front of the statute. "There, you see, my Lord," Daniel said to Nebuchadnezzar, pointing to the marble floor.

A fine layer of soot lay on the floor. Revealed in the ashes was the reason he had asked them to come no closer. There in the light of the guards' torches, several sets of footprints could be seen, all leading to a point behind the idol's base. Daniel took a torch from the soldier closest to him and shined its light on a small lever protruding from the right heel of the idol. He pulled the lever down, and a panel in the floor slid out of the way, revealing a staircase disappearing into the darkness below the idol.

"Naaman, send three of your men down there to see where the passageway leads," commanded Nebuchadnezzar. Turning to Haman, Nebuchadnezzar added, "Unless of course you care to spare us the trouble and tell us yourself."

Haman stood his ground, glaring back at Nebuchadnezzar, but not speaking. After a few minutes, one of the guards emerged from the chamber. "It leads to a passageway that goes to the south - do you wish us to follow it?"

"Yes, follow it, but I wager it will take you to Haman's quarters,"

Nebuchadnezzar barked. "Come, a surprise awaits you outside," Nebuchadnezzar said to the Chief Priest. As he led the way out of the idol, Naaman's guards brought Haman with them. The group emerged back into the sunlight, and found Timnah accompanied by a military escort waiting to greet them.

Naaman nodded his head to her, signaling that they had been successful in revealing Haman's secret passageway in the idol. Now, it was up to her to testify to what she knew. Naaman motioned for her to come forward. "My Lord," Naaman said turning to Nebuchadnezzar, "This is Timnah, the Queen of the Ashkelonites. Early on, Haman had forced her to do his bidding, and she cooperated against her will. But, since the attempted assassination of Belteshazzar, she has spied on Haman. She came to me and revealed that it was Haman who planned to have Daniel killed. He also conspired with the Edomites to have them attack our southern border while riots occurred here in the capitol. I bring her before you now as a witness to Haman's treachery."

Nebuchadnezzar walked over to where Timnah stood. "Is it as he says?" the king asked.

"Yes, my Lord. Haman has plotted against you from the beginning. Daniel has worked to keep the peace among the exiles and your own people. Haman wished Daniel dead, so that he would be able to fan the flames of your people's passions into a riot that would cause them to seek a new king. Haman would step forward, remove you, and restore order. He has said as much to me."

"Liar!" Haman hissed at Timnah.

Nebuchadnezzar ignored the Chief Priest. "Why would Haman share this with you?" Nebuchadnezzar asked.

"I was his mistress. Reuben, a Hebrew and Haman's servant, convinced me that a faction among the Hebrews wanted Daniel dead, that they would use their own people to commit the murder. I relayed a request from Reuben to Haman to arrange to have Daniel's guards leave their post to allow the assassins to do their job. Little did I realize that Haman had secretly devised a plan with Reuben to hire my own people as the killers." Timnah explained how Haman had had Reuben work with her own servant, Shala, to find assassins from her people to kill Daniel - how Haman came to have her signet ring which he used to forge orders from her so that it would be thought she had ordered her people to try to kill Daniel. Finally, she explained Haman's plan to use that incident to spark mass riots between the Hebrews and her people - how he had sought to distract the Babylonians from the invasion of warriors from Elam on Babylon's southern border that he secretly encouraged.

"My Lord," Timnah concluded, "You have the proof of his treachery before you. He has used this idol to fill his coffers at your expense. Why? To bind his followers closer to him, so that when he gave the word, they would rise up against you." Then, coming closer, so that he could feel her breath, she said, "You killed my father, king Ohlm of Ashkelon. Yet I have spoken with Daniel and Naaman and confessed what I know, instead of helping Haman. I now know that you are the true king ordained by the God of Heaven to rule the earth. That is why I testify against Haman, and not for him."

"Did you know this, Belteshazzar?" Nebuchadnezzar asked Daniel.

Daniel nodded his head in ascent, acknowledging he did.

"Yet you do not condemn her?"

"No, my Lord," replied Daniel.

"Then neither do I. Take Haman, his chief aides and his family and throw them to the lions."

"Now!" Haman bellowed. Twenty of his personal guard appeared from no where to challenge Naaman's soldiers. In the ensuing melee, Haman ran away.

Naaman looked up as he ran his sword through the gut of one of Haman's defenders to see the Chief Priest disappear down an alleyway. Glancing around, he saw that his men were having little trouble in dispatching their opponents. Assuring himself that Nebuchadnezzar, Daniel and Timnah were safely guarded, he took off to pursue Haman.

As he chased after his quarry, Naaman smiled to himself as he thought of the surprise Haman had in store when he encountered the blockade he had ordered to seal this section of the city. Every alley, street and rooftop was guarded against just such an escape attempt. Now that the Chief Priest's treachery had been revealed, Naaman's men would begin raiding every home and business of Haman's known supporters. By , Haman would be fed to the lions; in a week, all his supporters would follow.

Naaman rounded the corner of the building he had seen Haman pass. Though the narrow street was empty, he could hear footsteps up ahead around a curve. Naaman again took off sprinting, sword drawn, eyes scanning the buildings around him. Rounding the curve, he saw Haman attempting to climb a wall to reach the lower part of the stair-step rooftop. Naaman shouted, and watched as Haman, startled, lost his footing and fell to the ground, twisting his ankle.

"Argh!" Haman cried out in pain. He tried to stand, but couldn't. Naaman walked up to Haman and put his sword to the Chief Priest's throat.

"I have suspected for some time that you plotted against the King. Today, you die," Naaman said with satisfaction. With an expert thrust, he drove his sword through Haman's chest, and made sure he breathed his last. Then, taking Haman's sword which had fallen a few feet from him, replaced it in the dead Priest's outstretched hand. As his guards rounded the corner and came upon the scene, no one would question his need to kill Haman in self defense.

Naaman led his men, dragging Haman's dead body, back to the Temple of Beelzebub. "When I came upon him, he struck out at me, and would not submit. I was forced to kill him," he explained without emotion.

"Very good, Naaman," Nebuchadnezzar said, surveying the dead and dying around him. Looking at both Naaman and Timnah, he said, "I am in both your debts, and am ashamed for having allowed myself to be deluded by Haman's trickery. I will never doubt either of you again."

"Thank you, my Lord," replied Naaman, and turned to the task of tracking down Haman's supporters.

CHAPTER 23

The Hidden Prophecy of Isaiah

Wow, Grandpa. That was intense! But was Beelzebub a real god, or did you just make that up?"

"Oh, no! Here, lets turn to Matthew 12:22-26 in the Bible. You see, there was a man that Jesus cast a demon out of:

When the Pharisees heard about it, they said "This fellow does not cast out demons except by Beelzebub, the ruler of the demons." Jesus then replied to them this way, saying: " If Satan casts out Satan, he is divided against himself. How then will his kingdom stand?"

Grandpa closed his bible. "While I'm not sure where the name 'Beelzebub' came from, it was used to refer to an ancient Canaanite god. And so, for Jesus to be accused of being in league with Beelzebub was a terrible insult. I used that story to come up with the name of the god the bad guy, Haman, thought Daniel worshipped.

Isaiah nodded his head, and then asked another question. "So is any of the story of Daniel talking to King Nebuchadnezzar about the exposing the secret staircase in the idol actually in the bible?"

"Not in the bible, no," said Grandpa. "But it is in a book that is not part of the bible called the apocrypha. Now, a short story in that set of writings is a story called Bel and the Dragon. That's where you can find the basis of the story of the idol and the trap door, which Daniel uncovered using ashes on the floor." Grandpa removed his glasses to clean them.

Putting his glasses back on, Grandpa looked over at the pictures of his grandchildren on the refridgerator, and then looked back at his grandson. "Isaiah, when I was in third grade, there was a series of books I read about everything – ants, the planets, the human heart – all sorts of stuff. The series of books all began with the title 'All About The Human Heart' or whatever the topic was. Well, after reading those books, I thought I knew all about all those things." Grandpa paused, and then added "But guess what?"

"What?"

"When I got older I discovered there was much more detail about how the human heart works, and many other things that I had read in those 'All About' books. Details that would have been rather confusing to a third grader. Now, in the apocrypha, the story of Bel and the Dragon takes place when a man named Cyrus was king – not Nebuchadnezzar. And the story of Daniel in the Lions' Den doesn't happen when Nebuchadnezzar was king. It happens when a man named Darius ruled Babylon."

Isaiah looked down at the kitchen table and scratched at a crumb that had stuck to the table. Then, lifting his head, Isaiah said: "So what you're saying, Grandpa, is that there are some details you've left out to make the story simpler to tell to us, so we don't get confused with all these different kings. Right?"

Grandpa smiled and nodded his head. "That's right, Isaiah. You see, you are at an age now where you are ready to start reading and studying all sorts of things – including the bible – to learn things on your own. Finding it out for yourself, asking questions, and digging deeper, is a great way to learn anything in life. And, when you're ready to learn more, God will provide you a teacher who will help you unlock the secrets of any subject you choose to study.

Isaiah grinned. "Hey, it's like that line from the movie Zorro, with Antonio Baneras, when the old Zorro says "When the student is ready, the master will appear!"

Grandpa laughed heartily, remembering the line that Isaiah was referring to. "Yes, that old Zorro was played by Anthony Hopkins!" Grandpa cleared his throat and became more serious.

"Now, Isaiah, we're almost done. This last part of the story that I'm going to tell you involves another Old Testament prophet named Jeremiah. I have to tell you a little bit about him so that you can get an idea of how the whole story ends. In fact, when you're older, I hope you'll read a book called The Brotherhood of the Scroll. In that book, you'll learn more about the prophet Jeremiah, and the various kings of Judah, including one named Zedekiah. Are you ready for me to finish?"

> **Jeremiah the Prophet**
>
> As with the character, Troas, the prophet Jeremiah plays a very prominent role in **The Brotherhood of the Scroll**. Some have speculated that Jeremiah, in his early forties, knew both Daniel and Ezekiel, who would have been teenagers about the year 605 BC. Were they disciples of an older Jeremiah? We'll never know for sure. Visit www.wisejargon.com/brotherhood to learn more about the original novel, as well as a course designed to accompany the novel called **Clash of the Superpowers**.

"Let's do it, Grandpa!" said Isaiah.

And so, Grandpa put his glasses back on, turned to the last chapter of The Chronicles of Belteshazzar, and began to read:

Now it came about that in the ninth year of Zedekiah's reign, Nebuchadnezzar king of Babylon came and laid siege against Jerusalem for two years. Zedekiah sought the Lord, and tried to appease Him by releasing the bondservants. In the end, King Zedekiah trusted not in the Lord, but in Pharaoh. This was a false hope, one doomed to failure because of the alliance between Babylon and the Priests of Amun. Thus, Zedekiah did evil in the sight of the Lord just as Jehoiakim had done before him, and the Captain of King Nebuchadnezzar's guard broke down all the walls of Jerusalem, and took her people into exile.

The Chronicles of Belteshazzar

Jeremiah lay in an unfamiliar bed, propped up with cushions, and leaned forward to take a small sip from a steaming cup of herbal tea. Weakened from over two months of imprisonment, the Prophet of the Lord endured a momentary state of consciousness. He longed for sleep to come again and relieve him of the memories of these past several months, to no avail. Once again, the tears began to flow. Covering his face with his hands, Jeremiah once again relived the events that had led to this ...

Jeremiah came as he had been requested to meet Zedekiah at the city gate. It had been only a couple of days since the Babylonians had left to fight the Egyptians. The King had greeted him and asked him to pray for the city, but he would have none of it. Instead, he had declared to Zedekiah and all his priests the message the Lord had given him.

"The Lord God of Israel says to the King of Judah: 'Pharaoh's army, though it came here to help you, is about to return in flight to Egypt! The Babylonians shall defeat them and send them scurrying home. These Babylonians shall capture this city and burn it to the ground. Don't fool yourselves into believing the Babylonians are gone for good. They aren't! Even if you destroyed their entire army until there was only a handful of survivors and they lay wounded in their tents, yet they would stagger out and defeat you and put this city to the torch'."

Zedekiah had turned red with embarrassment, and commanded him to leave. Within two weeks, the Babylonians had returned to renew the siege, crushing the hopes of the Hebrews. Just before they had returned, Jeremiah had received word that he was needed in Anathoth to settle some issues with the family estate. But when he had tried to leave, a guard captain had arrested him, accusing him of spying for the Babylonians.

Though Jeremiah had protested that he was not spying, the guard had not listened. He had been taken to the city officials. They were incensed with Jeremiah and had him whipped and put into a pit. There he had remained for several days, until Zedekiah had him come secretly to the palace. The King asked if there was any new word from the Lord. "Only that you shall be defeated by the king of Babylon," Jeremiah had replied. But instead of being sent back to the pit, Zedekiah ordered him sent to the palace prison instead.

Jeremiah started, awaking from his dream - the prison walls! They had seemed so real. He reached out to grasp the cup of herbal tea, now cold to the touch. Without seeming to notice the liquid had grown cold, Jeremiah drank deeply, until the cup was empty. Putting the cup down, he noticed that someone had brought some bread and cheese for him while he had slept. Realizing he was famished, Jeremiah ate his fill in silence.

His meal done, Jeremiah had nothing to distract him from his thoughts. To think that his own people had called him a traitor ...

"We have just come from the King. We told him you're a traitor, and guess what? He's washed his hands of the whole affair. No longer will your words weaken the will of our warriors, prophet! Tonight, you descend into Sheol."

A small group of priests had come to where he was being kept under arrest in the palace, dragging him to one of the city cisterns. Designed to store water, the drought that had fallen on the land had left it a muddy pit. They threw Jeremiah into the cistern, leaving him there to rot.

But not long after they had left, a black man had come to rescue him. Along with some others, he lowered a rope to Jeremiah and pulled him out of the cistern, after which they returned him to the palace jail. Jeremiah had lost all track of time, but knew it would not be long before the Babylonians breached Jerusalem's walls. Once again, King Zedekiah had sent for him, to ask if the Lord would rescue him.

He had known that the King would not listen, but answered him anyway. "The Lord, the God of Hosts, says: 'If you will surrender to Babylon, you and your family shall live and the city will not be burned. If you refuse to surrender, this city shall be set afire by the Babylonians, and you shall not escape.'"

In the end, Zedekiah had been more afraid of the Hebrews who wanted him to fight than of what might happen were he to surrender. After that, Jeremiah was again returned to the palace prison, where he remained until the day Jerusalem fell.

Jeremiah sat up in bed, his skin clammy with sweat. He could not get the sight of the Temple, in flames, out of his mind. It was true! The Lord had destroyed Israel like an enemy. He had destroyed her forts and palaces; He had destroyed the Temple as though it were a booth of dry leaves and branches.

"My God!" Jeremiah cried out. "I have cried until the tears will no longer come. My heart is broken, my spirit poured out. What shall we do?" With that, Jeremiah was overcome by a wracking cough. He barely noticed that another had entered the room.

"Here, Jeremiah. Drink this," said Gedaliah as he offered the prophet fresh tea. "Don't despair, my teacher. There is one ray of hope. Remember when you sent me out to prepare our people for this time, a remnant of the faithful? I have done so. The Babylonians have taken our leaders into captivity, but there are still those who believe in the Lord. Baruch and I have spoken with the Babylonian commander, Naaman, as you had asked us to do. He has made me the Governor, to rule our people as a representative of Nebuchadnezzar. So you see, all your work in leading the Brotherhood of the Scroll to preserve the Word of God has not been in vain."

"That is good news," Jeremiah weakly replied, lying back on the cushions. "And the King, Zedekiah? What of his fate?"

Gedaliah smiled, tears welling up in his eyes. "He tried to escape, and fled toward Jericho. The Babylonians captured him near there, and have taken him in chains to Nebuchadnezzar at Riblah. I don't know if he lives or not."

Jeremiah looked away from Gedaliah. So, after all this time, after all his warnings, Zedekiah would now pay the price of disobedience. But at least Gedaliah would rebuild their hopes here. And in Babylon, Daniel and Ezekiel would prepare the hearts of their people to await their restoration to Jerusalem. He took another sip of the tea Gedaliah had brought, and drifted back off to sleep.

From his chamber in the Tower of Etemenanki, Daniel stood, looking out over the city of Babylon, the events of the last few days overwhelming him. After having been gone for nearly two years, Naaman had returned with over two thousand captives brought from Jerusalem. Among them was Zedekiah, who only yesterday died in Nebuchadnezzar's dungeon. The poor man! Naaman had taken the King of Judah to Nebuchadnezzar at Riblah. There, the Babylonian sovereign had pronounced sentence. Before his very eyes, Zedekiah's two sons were brought before him and slain. Next, Nebuchadnezzar ordered Zedekiah's eyes put out. Half dragged on the journey back to Babylon, Zedekiah was nearly dead when he arrived. His death ended this chapter of Judah's rebellion and humiliation. A new one was about to unfold.

New beginnings. That thought brought a tired smile to Daniel's face. Naaman had come home to find Timnah and their son, now seven months old. Naaman had said, "At last, I know that there is no other God in all the world except the God of the Hebrews. Never again will I offer offerings to any god except the Lord Jehovah."

Naaman had asked one thing only: That because of his position in Nebuchadnezzar's court, that at the Feast of Akitu, when all Babylonians were to bow to Marduk and the king, that he be forgiven for doing so. Daniel had taken Naaman's hand and, smiling, simply said "Go in peace." Yes, God was about to do a new thing, and Naaman's conversion, though secret, was but one example. All those years ago, Jeremiah had formed a "Brotherhood of the Scroll" to plan for this day. It had finally arrived. This evening, Daniel would explain the secrets that God had unlocked for him, and the promise those secrets held.

Below him, Daniel saw Ezekiel, Meshach, Shadrach and Abednego begin to ascend the steps to join him. It would not be long before he could finally reveal to them what was about to unfold.

Inside his chamber, Daniel had prepared wine and bread to serve his friends. The four sat in silence, as Daniel served them and then cleared away the remains. Finally, with an oil lamp burning above him, Daniel broke the silence.

"Years ago," Daniel began, "during the feast of Akitu, when they forced our people to bow to the gods of the Babylonians, I went into the mountains to pray. Ezekiel went with me. One night, I had a terrifying dream in which I was with the three of you, walking around in a furnace. Until this night, I have not spoken of it with anyone."

"It was you, Daniel? You rescued us from Haman's furnace?" asked Meshach, speaking for the three survivors of the furnace.

"Not I. No, it was the Lord," Daniel replied. "He only allowed me to witness His miracle. I drew strength from that vision which allowed me to face the truths which He has shown me. It is time for me to now share those truths with you."

Walking over to a curtain covering a portion of the northern wall of the chamber, Daniel slid the curtain back to reveal a map of the known world. "Having friends in high places allows you to see the inside details of how Nebuchadnezzar runs his kingdom," Daniel began. "As you know, the great trade route between Egypt and Babylon runs through Judah by the Way of the Sea. Caravans travel through there north to Carchemish, and then follow the Euphrates south here to Babylon. From here, goods can then be put on boats and shipped out through the Gulf of Persia and eastward to India. Thus, by controlling Palestine and the Gaza Plain, including our homeland, Nebuchadnezzar can exact any duty he wishes on trade passing from east to west."

"But, that is not the only trade caravan route. To the north are the peoples of Gomar, Rosh, and the Scythians, who live along the border of the Black Sea. King Cyraxes of Media wishes to control that trade route, and has been slowly expanding his kingdom in that region. Nebuchadnezzar has struck a bargain with Cyraxes - Nebuchadnezzar seeking control of the southern trade route tracking the Great Sea to Egypt, Cyraxes the control of the trade route passing north to the Black Sea."

"That explains why Nebuchadnezzar took Amythis, one of Cyraxes's daughters, for a wife over a year ago," Ezekiel observed.

"You're right. It is because of this alliance that I learned about a boy named Cyrus. He is the grandson of Astyages, a general under the command of Cyraxes, King of Media. He lives in one of Media's conquered territories, in a city called Persepolis. He is yet a lad, but will come to play an important roll in the future of our people."

Daniel walked over to an alcove in the wall where he hid his most prized possessions. From its recesses, he withdrew the scrolls which his father had given him when he left Jerusalem years ago. Carrying them over to a nearby table, Daniel unrolled one of them.

"Years ago, the Prophet Jeremiah charged us with forming a sacred Brotherhood of the Scroll, to protect and preserve the Word of God. As I studied these scrolls," Daniel began, "I came to realize that God had appointed this Cyrus for a special task. For years, I have known that Jerusalem and the Temple of Solomon would be destroyed, and that this Cyrus would order it rebuilt." Daniel paused until he found the passage for which he had been looking. "Here, listen to these words:"

It is I who says of Cyrus, "He is My shepherd! And he will perform all My desire." And he declares of Jerusalem, "She will be built," And of the temple, "Your foundation will be laid." Thus says the Lord to Cyrus His anointed: "God shall empower his right hand and he shall crush the strength of mighty kings. God shall open the gates of Babylon to you; I will shatter the doors of bronze, and cut through their iron bars. And I will give you the treasures of darkness, and hidden wealth of secret places, in order that you may know it is I, The Lord, the God of Israel, who calls you by name."

"But Isaiah wrote this over one hundred years ago," Ezekiel whispered, his face registering the meaning of what Daniel had just read. The Temple had stood for nearly four hundred years. Therefore, if it were to be rebuilt, it must first be destroyed - an event which had been only recently accomplished by Nebuchadnezzar's army. "How long have you known this?"

Daniel rolled up the scroll to return it to its hiding place. "For about six years, I have known that the Temple would be destroyed. Since learning this, I have searched for signs of the coming of the one called Cyrus. Years ago, my father taught me how to search the sacred scrolls for revelations from God not clearly evident in the text. By laying out the text of the Torah in ten-by-ten arrays, I could eliminate the spaces between the words. The more I studied in this way, the more I was able to see that there are patterns hidden therein. For example, I found several references to the ninth day of Ab ..."

"The day the Temple was destroyed!" interrupted Shadrach.

"Precisely," answered Daniel. "And there is more. Using the mathematics of the Babylonians, I have been able to calibrate with exact precision the length of the lunar month: 29.53059 days. I have been able to calculate the next great eclipse of the sun. It will happen in less than a year, on the day that Cyrus will turn 15."

"Will Cyrus become king of the Medes at that time?" asked Ezekiel.

"I don't know. All I can guess is that it will mark a turning point in his life - a life that will culminate in the redemption of our people. God told Jeremiah that our people would live in captivity for seventy years. Less than a third of that time has passed. Until the time for which our God has appointed Cyrus has come, we must help our people to be faithful. Only by staying true to our God will our people be prepared to return to Jerusalem and rebuild the Temple when the time is right."

Daniel paused, smiling at his friends before continuing. "I know that this is a great burden, but it is one which has been entrusted into our hands. For now, no one else must know what I have told you. In time, we will share this knowledge with those who will come after us. We must make more copies of the sacred scrolls which I have here. I will train you in the ways of studying its hidden meanings - the secret of the 'wheels within wheels.' Will you agree to this?"

The four looked at him, and nodded their heads in assent. Daniel smiled and closed his eyes. The Lord had shown him so much in the years since he had come to Babylon. And though Daniel knew some of what was yet to come, the details of that future were far from written. What kind of a man this Cyrus would be, and whether or not he would ever even meet this conquering king, he did not know. For now, at least, the Lord had shown him a way to begin.

And that was enough.

CHAPTER 24

Questions

WAVE GOODBYE TO Nai Nai and Grandpa!" The four children yelled and waved to their grandparents as Auntie Dr. Sarah backed the car out of her parents' driveway. The two waved goodbyes to their grandchildren as she slowly turned the corner to begin to exit the neighborhood. She would have the kids for the next hour as she drove them home to her brother and sister-in-law's home.

Beside her sat Isaiah, while the younger three sat in the back seat. Only Hope required a booster seat. My, how the laws about car seats had changed since she was a child, Sarah thought! She'd borrowed this one from her brother Jason, as she seldom had need to drive the children. It was so good having them around so she could also spend time with them!

Sarah looked at Isaiah and asked, "Well, did you get your question about 'separation between church and state' answered?" She returned her attention to the road as she awaited her nephew's response.

"Yes, I did. I know a whole lot more than I did before!" Isaiah squirmed a little in his seat, and then asked a question that he'd been wrestling with. "Do you think I ought to go talk to Mary about what I learned."

"Depends on how you do it," replied his aunt. "Do you plan to do it in a mean way, or as a way to start up a conversation with her?"

"Well, I don't want to be mean about it. How do you think I should bring it up?"

Auntie Dr. Sarah smiled and said with a wink. "Sometimes girls do what Mary did because they actually like the boy they are teasing. So, this might be a way for you to get to know her better. You might start out by telling her that you'd done some thinking about what she said. Now, she might have totally forgotten the topic. She might ask you what you mean, and then you can say that if she'll let you buy her a coke at McDonalds, you can tell her what you learned about 'separation between church and state,' and maybe even about the story of Daniel."

"Isaiah's got a girlfriend, Isaiah's got a girlfriend!" Nadia started chanting from the back seat. Isaiah turned a little red at his sister's taunting.

Auntie Dr. Sarah interrupted and said "Isaiah's just going to find a way to share what he learned and make a new friend. Now, what about the rest of you? Tell me all about your weekend with Nai Nai and Grandpa. Did you have fun? Did Grandpa tell you stories?"

Hope spoke first. "Nai Nai played with me and read me books while Grandpa told stories to the big kids. I got tired of listening to him."

"She also made us popcorn and we had some ice cream" added Josiah. "I stayed up with Isaiah and Nadia to listen to Grandpa, but then I got tired and fell asleep"

Nadia chimed in. "There weren't many girls in his story, but one of them was a woman named Timnah. She was one of Daniel's enemies at first. But then, she realized he wasn't bad like she thought he was. In the end, she decided to help Daniel and Naaman. But I'm not sure what happened, because I finally fell asleep during that part of Grandpa's story."

"Well, I stayed awake for the whole thing. Once Nai Nai, Nadia and Josiah were asleep, Grandpa and I went out into the kitchen to have a snack and finish the story." Isaiah paused for a moment, then asked: "Auntie Dr. Sarah, do you think Timnah was a real person?"

"Hmph!" responded his aunt. "Absolutely not! Timnah is a fictional character. Grandpa came up with her name because that's the name of the town where Sampson's first wife came from."

"I thought Sampson's wife was named Delilah."

"That was the name of Sampson's second wife, Isaiah." Auntie Dr. Sarah paused to check traffic patterns as she merged into traffic on I 70 off the interstate highway ramp. "Sampson's first wife was also a Philistine, and she came from a town called Timnah not far for the ancient Philistine city of Ashkelon. And do you know who Grandpa based Timnah's appearance on so that she would look like that woman?"

"I'll bet it was you!" chimed in Nadia from the back seat.

"You're right, Nadia. And let me tell you, I was not happy with your grandpa when I found that out! I didn't like the idea of having a devious, scheming evil woman based on me, even if she wasn't a real person!"

"But in the end, she turned out to be a brave woman who did the right thing, just like you always do."

Sarah looked at Isaiah and lightened up as she saw the sincere look on his face. Coughing slightly, she nodded her head and then said: "Anything else you all had questions about from Grandpa's story?"

Isaiah scrunched up his eyes as he thought about the question he wanted to ask. "At the end of the story, Daniel had a meeting with some of his friends in a building that looks like a pyramid. It's called a Ziggurat. Daniel talked about a group he called "The Brotherhood of the Scroll" that would protect and preserve the ancient scrolls that had been written by prophets like Isaiah. Was The Brotherhood of the Scroll a real group?"

Auntie Dr. Sarah laughed. "The Brotherhood of the Scroll is a novel Grandpa wrote back in the late 1990s. The story you heard him tell is what is called an "abbreviated version" of that book. While the group of Daniel and his friends is fictional, we know that somebody had to have preserved all the writings of the ancient Hebrews. Whether it was Daniel and his friends, or some other group of unknown Hebrews that preserved those ancient scrolls and made copies of them, I don't know."

"I didn't know Grandpa had written books before. That's cool!" Isaiah paused for a few seconds to gather his thoughts, then asked one more question. "Ok, there was this other guy that Daniel talked about in the story. A boy by the name of Cyrus. In the story, Daniel said he had predicted when the next eclipse of the sun would be, and that the eclipse would happen when this Cyrus kid turned 15 years old. Was this Cyrus guy a real person, and was Daniel actually good enough at astronomy that he could predict things like when an eclipse would happen?"

Sarah thought for a few moments. Astronomy was not something she knew a lot about, but then she remembered that the Babylonian Magi had been expert astronomers. After gathering her thoughts, she said to Isaiah; "Well, you remember that Nebuchadnezzar put Daniel in charge of all the Wise Men. They were called 'The Magi'."

"Yes, I remember," said Isaiah.

"So, whether it was Daniel, or one of the Magi who worked for him, it is very likely that they could have predicted when the next total eclipse of the sun would happen. Now, I remember Grandpa telling me about a famous battle that was fought in central Turkey in a place called Cappadocia."

At the mention of Cappadocia, Nadia piped up. "Hey, we visited Cappadocia back when Dad was working as a missionary in Turkey. That was really cool! They have lots of hot air balloons that you can go up in the air and look down on these rock houses that are called – what are they called, Isaiah?"

"Fire Chimneys. They were created by a huge ancient volcano like a million years ago."

"Well, kids, it looks like you are way ahead of me on this subject, then. But getting back to your question, Isaiah, there was a battle that was fought there in the central part of what is now modern Turkey. You know what the battle was called?"

"Nope," replied Isaiah, and waited for his aunt to tell him.

"Well," she said, "it was called The Battle of the Eclipse."

"The Battle of the Eclipse?" said Josiah. "Like the kind of battle you fight with swords and chariots? Tell us about it, Auntie Dr. Sarah, please, please, please!!!"

Sarah laughed at Josiah's pleading request. "Sorry, I can't do that. I've told you all I know. You'll just have to ask Grandpa about that the next time you see him.

"Well, I can't wait that long. I want to find out about that battle. I'm going to use Dad's computer to google it as soon as we get home." And with that, Isaiah stopped asking questions and looked out the window, wishing that the car would go faster.

Epilogue

THAT WAS SOME story, Isaiah." Mary grabbed her book bag from where it lay against the park bench where they had been sitting. They had begun the story at the Soda Shop, but finished their milk shakes several hours ago and had walked to the local park. "Let's walk home. I live that way." She pointed in the direction of her house.

They had walked for half a block when Mary asked, "Is your grandfather going to tell you more stories? It sounds like that Cyrus guy who was prophesied about was a mysterious person."

Isaiah shrugged his shoulders. "I don't know, but I can ask him next time I see him."

Mary nodded, then asked a different question. "So, did you look up that Battle of the Eclipse?"

Isaiah smiled and laughed. "Of course! It was fought during a full eclipse of the sun. The two kingdoms fought the battle in what is today the country of Turkey. They decided the eclipse was some sort of sign from the gods that they should stop fighting each other and make peace." Isaiah hesitated, and then continued. "History records that two observers from Babylon came and watched the battle. Evidently, their astronomers had predicted right when the eclipse would happen. They had the prince and the princess of the two countries marry each other to end the war."

Mary smiled, nodded, and then looking up at Isaiah said, "Wouldn't it be crazy if Daniel was one of the Babylonians who went to where the battle was fought to negotiate the peace? Do you think he did that?"

Isaiah shrugged his shoulders. "I don't know. Anything's possible, I guess."

They kept walking, making small talk about school. And then, Mary said, "This is my house. Bend down. I want to tell you a secret of my own."

Isaiah, a frown of confusion contorting his face, bent down as Mary tugged his ear close to her lips. "Your aunt was right!" She kissed him on the cheek and quickly went inside the house.

Isaiah paused a moment, turned, and started running, grinning all the way home.

About the Author

David Lantz is married to his wife Sally. They have three children, as well as four grandchildren. He is an Adjunct College Professor of Economics and self-published author. David was named the 2005 Faculty of the Year by the first graduating class of the Indianapolis Campus of the University of Phoenix. In addition to the fiction and non-fiction books he has written, David has also created a series of courses related to entrepreneurship, teaching online, and Christian ministry. **The Chronicles of Belteshazzar** is based on his earlier novel, **The Brotherhood of the Scroll**. You can learn more about these books by visiting his website at ***www.wisejargon.com/brotherhood***.

To learn how to order additional copies of The Chronicles of Belteshazzar, either in e-book, soft or hard cover formats, please visit ***www.wisejargon.com/chronicles***.